ROCK GOD

The Legend of B.J. Levine

ROCK GOD

The Legend of B.J. Levine

Barnabas Miller

Cover art and design by Sammy Yuen
Cover images © Thinkstock

Published by Sourcebooks Jabberwocky, an imprint of Sourcebooks, Inc.
P.O. Box 4410, Naperville, Illinois 60567-4410
(630) 961-3900
Fax: (630) 961-2168
www.jabberwockykids.com

Library of Congress Cataloging-in-Publication data is on file with the publisher.

Source of Production: Webcom, Toronto, Canada
Date of Production: November 2011
Run Number: 16403

Printed and bound in Canada.
WC 10 9 8 7 6 5 4 3 2 1

For Heidi, who truly rocks

Dear Sammy,

Hi, it's me, Nigel. I mean, not Nigel, but I'll explain that in a second.

Sammy, I'm writing to find out if you are okay. Are you okay? And also, where are you? You took off so fast, I didn't get a chance to say goodbye to you, so I have to write you this letter because I'm not supposed to talk to you, and you don't have an email address, and there are some way important things I need to tell you.

First of all, I wanted to let you know that because of you, I have officially decided to become an all-powerful god of rock. Not just a rock musician but a full-on, fire-breathing MEGALORD OF RRRRROCK. I know this won't be easy (yes, Mom will still try to make me wear the wrinkle-proof Dockers and the loafers with the actual pennies in them), but I've got to try, Sammy. I've got to try. Second of all, you told me that if I wanted to become a full-on, fire breathing MEGALORD OF RRRRROCK, I would have to speak the Truth with a capital T, and I think I finally know what you mean.

So, I'm writing to tell you the Truth, Sammy. The whole Truth about me. A lot of it will sound pretty freaky, especially when I get to the part about the ancient tribe of grandpas in tight leather pants and bandannas who are trying to kill me. That is the part you probably won't believe, but I swear it's true, even if you think I'm psycho. There are a bunch of evil rock and roll grandpas who want me dead. Or maybe they want me dead or alive, I'm not really sure. To be honest, I can't really tell the good guys from the bad guys yet, but I know I can trust you, Sammy, so here it is. The Truth about me with a capital T.

First of all, remember at the beginning of the letter when I said that I wasn't Nigel? Well, that is the first thing I need to tell you. My real name is not Nigel "Hot Wings" Thunderdome. You probably knew that since it doesn't sound like a real name. My real name is B.J. Levine, which sounds way less rockin' than Nigel "Hot Wings" Thunderdome, but my mom won't let me change it. Also, I think I should tell you that I am not really from Hillshire Farms, England. You probably knew that too since Hillshire Farms is a smoked breakfast sausage. Plus, you've toured all over the world, so you probably know that there's no Hillshire Farms, England. I really wish I had come up with something better, but it was the most English-sounding name I could come up with at the time, and also I was thinking a lot about smoked sausage after Terry the Wunder-Dwarf cooked up all that bacon at the show.

Look, Sammy, the truth is...I'm from Cleveland. Yes, Cleveland, Ohio. I know. Boring. But I just moved to Greenwich Village in New York City, and that's a lot less boring, right? At least it's closer to England.

Really, I think the truest thing I can say about my life is that the first thirteen years have been super boring. More boring than I even realized. It turns out my life didn't really start until about two weeks ago. That was the day we moved to New York, and that was the day this total freak named Merv showed up at our new house.

Now, Sammy, this is really important. You need to be on the lookout for Merv. He looks kind of like a hundred-year-old old biker dude,but more like one of those hobo wizards from that '80s band ZZ Top. Do you know ZZ Top? I think they have a song on Guitar Hero III. Wait, what am I saying? Of course you know ZZ Top. You know like every band in the world ever. Well, Merv looks kind of like one of them, so you've gotta keep your eyes open. He wears a dusty old leather jacket, a red bandanna, and these really tight leather pants. He has a long, scraggly red beard and these bulging, bloodshot eyes. His eyes are what scared me to death when he showed up at my house, especially when he asked to talk to my dad. The weird thing was that my dad actually talked to Merv—like really talked to him—which was so strange because my dad doesn't really talk to anyone that much. He just kind of mumbles and strums his guitar, and—

Wait. This letter isn't making any sense, right? Now I'm going way too fast. I told you I was a lousy writer.

Okay, all you really need to know about my dad is this: Dad only cares about two things. He cares about his guitars, and he cares about his quilt. Yes, you read that right. My dad is in love with a big orange quilt. He had it nailed to the wall of our basement in Cleveland, but the second we walked into our new house, he just dropped all his bags, dug into his suitcase, and pulled out that quilt. He had it all carefully folded inside a million pounds of plastic wrap. He unwrapped it really slowly and tacked it up on our new kitchen wall like it was the only piece of furniture we needed. See, the whole thing about my dad's quilt is that it's got his favorite song lyric sewn on it in big black letters. It's the same song lyric we talked about, Sammy, and I'm telling you right now, I still think it is the dumbest lyric I have ever heard.

But that's really where I should start my story. I should start with the crazy quote on Dad's quilt. Because I was reading it the morning Merv showed up at my house and changed my life.

CHAPTER one

It still didn't make any sense. No matter how many times B.J. read the quote on the kitchen wall, he could not make heads or tails of it.

He knew that it came from a song called "Wanted Dead or Alive" by his father's idol, Mr. Jon Bon Jovi, a world famous rocker and possibly a gunslinger from the Wild West. But everything else about the quote was an impenetrable mystery.

For one thing, in the first line, Mr. Bon Jovi said that he carried around a "loaded six string" and B.J. knew for a fact that there was no such thing as this mythical half-gun/half-guitar. But far more confusing was the last line, where Mr. Bon Jovi claimed that he'd "seen a million faces and rocked them all."

Just how exactly do you rock a face? That was all B.J. wanted to know. What does it look like when someone's face gets rocked? Does it hurt? Is it awesome? Or is it contagious, like with zombies?

Like, once your face gets rocked, do you fall into a cold, dead trance and try to chase some poor guy down the street so you can rock *his* face? And what if you don't want your face to be rocked? Can you *un*rock a face in an emergency? And did Jon Bon Jovi really rock *all* one million faces he saw? Isn't it more likely that he missed one or two faces along the way?

And what was the big deal with the quote on the quilt anyway? Why was Dad so obsessed with it? And why did he insist on hanging it over the new breakfast nook if he didn't want to talk about it?

B.J.'s head was spinning with these questions and many more, but asking his father to answer them was as hopeless as ever. This may have been a brand-new city and a brand-new kitchen, but the breakfast conversation hadn't changed one bit since Cleveland.

"Come on, Dad," B.J. groaned, his mouth full of Cap'n Crunch. "Just answer the question."

"Whatever, Beej," his father replied as he sliced more banana chunks onto his peanut butter and banana sandwich.

"No, not 'whatever,' Dad. That's not an answer. Just tell me. *How* do you rock a face? Why won't you just tell me? I still don't get it. Does Mr. Bon Jovi have a gun on his back or is it a guitar? It doesn't make any sense." B.J. pointed at the sunlit quilt, his hand following along its embroidered black letters like he was reading from the chalkboard in class. "Look, he says he's got a '*loaded* six-string on his back,' but a guitar doesn't use any bullets, Dad, so how can it be loaded?"

"Okay, Beej."

"And a gun doesn't have six strings. It doesn't have any strings, so what is he carrying on his back? Is it a gun or is it a guitar? Which is it, Dad? And who *is* this guy anyway?"

B.J.'s father dropped his banana onto his plate and fell into a long, drawn-out silence. His platinum blond hair was tied back in a ponytail behind his slim, chiseled face, and he was wearing his aviator sunglasses at the breakfast table again, so there was no way to see his eyes. B.J. wasn't sure if he'd annoyed his father into a sudden vegetative state or if Dad had just decided to take a quick power nap at the breakfast table. Sometimes it was hard to tell whether he was awake or asleep behind his shades because he said so little. Jayson "Hot Wings" Levine was a man of few words. It was only when he began to pluck out a little melody on his acoustic guitar that B.J. knew for sure that he was awake. Dad always strummed his guitar at the breakfast table. He also strummed it at the dinner table, the coffee table, and every other table in the house.

"Dad…? Dad, are you still listening to me?"

"Uh-huh, uh-huh," his father replied. Only now he was singing the word "uh-huh." He was singing it over and over again: "*Uh-huh, uh-huh, uh-huh…*"

He was not, in fact, listening. No, he had officially floated off to that little rock and roll universe in his mind where he wrote his songs. B.J. should have recognized the "uh-huh" song—Dad had been working on it for the last six weeks. Now he was singing it ten times louder than he ever had before.

"Uh-huh, uh-huh, uh-huh. Just run for the border!
Uh-huh, uh-huh, uh-huh. It's a new world order!

"No!" Dad stomped his bare foot down on the floor. "No, that's all wrong. New world order? That's horrible." He re-tuned, and pounded away at the strings again. "*Uh-huh, uh-huh, uh-huh. Just run for the border...*"

"Dad..."

"*Uh-huh, uh-huh, uh-huh...*"

"Dad...?"

"*You're a TACO SNORTER. BAD chihuahua, don't SNORT the TACO, don't SNORT the TACOOOOO!*"

"Dad, can you please stop playing the Taco Bell song for a minute?"

"It's not about Taco Bell. It's about a war between dogs in the future. *Uh-huh, uh-huh...*"

Thank God, a pounding at the back door finally interrupted Dad's masterpiece. Dad jumped up from his chair and swung open the back door, and there was chubby little Kevin Hammond—B.J.'s best friend in the world and quite possibly his only chance for survival in New York.

Kev and B.J. had been best friends since kindergarten. Their mothers worked for the accounting firm of Emerson, Lake, and Tuschman and had been promoted to new jobs in the New York office, so the families had moved east together. The Hammonds had found a brownstone right next to the Levines' on Perry Street, so B.J.'s best friend was now his next-door neighbor too. There was just one problem: Kevin had another best friend in New York, and his name was Jayson "Hot Wings" Levine.

"What *up*, Kev?" Dad gave Kevin a morning fist bump. "*Qué pasa, hombre?* You got time for a quick game of GH3 before school?"

"Oh, you know it, Mr. L.," Kevin grinned. "If you've got the bass gee-tar, I've got the time!"

This was the problem: Kevin was an incredibly gifted bass player, especially for a thirteen-year-old. He said it was part of his African American heritage—his grandpa was a Mississippi blues man and his father was a "master of funk" back in college. He'd literally been born to play the bass. B.J., on the other hand, came from four generations of accountants on his mother's side, dating back to a family of Russian sheep-counters in Minsk. He had not inherited any of his father's musical genes. He had been born to do taxes.

"Wassup, Beej!" Kev hollered. "Are you ready for some NYC?" He gave B.J. a hard slap on the back as he bounded into the kitchen, but within seconds, Kev and Dad had disappeared into the half-furnished living room for a game of Guitar Hero III. They played it every time Kevin came over—Dad on guitar, Kevin on bass, B.J. on nothing. Apparently, they were going to carry on the tradition in New York, and that left B.J. with a slightly nauseous ache in his stomach. He sank deeper into his chair as the sound of screeching guitars erupted from the living room.

Mom burst into the kitchen, shoving a stack of overstuffed manila folders into her briefcase. She looked tall and lanky in her new suit, and she'd combed all her short jet-black hair over to the side—probably to make her soccer mom haircut look a little more New York–ish.

"Are they playing without you again, sweetie?" She ruffled his hair on her way to the coffee maker. "Don't worry. I'll go break up their game in two minutes, okay?"

"Nah, it's cool," B.J. mumbled, staring at his soggy cereal. "Let 'em play. I'm fine. I'm going to go change for school."

He stood up from his chair and dragged his feet slowly down the hall, passing the airy living room on his way to the stairs. He stopped and stared at Dad and Kevin moshing triumphantly to Guns N' Roses' "Welcome to the Jungle" on their little plastic guitars. Kevin took a running jump into a long knee-slide across the newly varnished floor while Dad bounced up and down like a pogo stick, thrashing his long platinum hair back and forth like a horse's mane. The longer B.J. stared at them, the more the harsh reality set in: *This might as well be Cleveland.*

For some reason, he'd thought things would be different in New York—he thought everything was going to change—but who was he kidding? Every day would be exactly the same as the day before: Dad on guitar, Kevin on bass, B.J. on nothing.

When the doorbell rang, B.J. figured it was Mrs. Hammond joining Mom for coffee before work, so he stepped into the foyer and swung open the front door without even asking who it was.

And then he screamed. He screamed like a little girl. Or not exactly like a little girl—more like some sort of frightened monkey. Like a frightened, heavy metal–singing monkey who'd just stepped on a rusty nail. Unfortunately, no one heard his wild monkey scream because it was drowned out by the pterodactyl-like squawks of Guns N' Roses' lead singer, Axl Rose. No one had even heard the doorbell ring. So B.J. stood alone in the windy foyer, gazing at the ghoulish, leather-clad stranger in the doorway.

The pale figure was definitely human, but he looked less like a man than some kind of ancient, wheezing, biker creature in tight leather pants. His grizzled face was just as leathery as his jacket, and the wispy gray hairs sticking out from under his red bandanna looked more like quills than regular old-man hair. His long red beard was as bristly as goat hair. Even after he pulled off his dark wrap-around sunglasses, B.J. couldn't guess how old the biker creature was.

They stared at each other in silence—B.J. panting in fear and the old man wheezing like a caged bull. Finally, after blinking his goggle eyes repeatedly, the old man spoke.

"I am Merv," he said.

He announced it as if it were very important. As if no other name could possibly have the same impact as his. He wasn't some random Joey or Mike from down the street. He was *Merv.*

B.J. took an involuntary step back when he heard Merv's deep, gravelly voice. This may have been the first time he'd spoken in a hundred years. His accent didn't sound like the other New York accents B.J. had heard. He sounded more like one of those guidos from *Jersey Shore*. But it was Merv's tattoos that really paralyzed B.J. Particularly the tattoo on the side of his neck: a pointy-fingered hand making the sign of the devil horns. It wasn't that B.J. feared that Merv might be Satan. He was just mildly concerned that Merv might have *worked* for Satan at some point in time.

"May I come in?" Merv asked.

B.J. couldn't bring himself to speak, so he did the only logical thing he could think to do next. He slammed the door in Merv's face and tried to run for his mommy.

★ ★ ★

"Hey!" Merv slammed his hand against the front door before B.J. could close it all the way. "Listen to me, circus boy! Nobody slams the door on Merv!"

B.J.'s stomach jumped into his throat as Merv stomped into the foyer uninvited. Dad and Kevin had just started jamming on the Beastie Boys' "Sabotage," so they still couldn't hear B.J. struggling to fend off the biker hobo creature.

"Now, where is he?" Merv growled. "I need to speak with Levine."

"What?" B.J.'s fingers and toes went numb. Had the demon hobo come for *him*?

"Le-*vine*," Merv barked. "I *need* to speak with Hot Wings Levine, and I need to speak with him *right now*."

"Wait...Hot Wings? You know my dad?"

"*HOT WIIIIIIINGS!*" Merv cried out from some deep, rumbling place at the base of his diaphragm. He'd clearly run out of patience with B.J.'s games. "Hot Wings Levine, I know you are here, man! I *found* you, man, and I know you're here. I can hear you playing that wussy Beastie Boys crap! You get your butt out here right now, Hot Wings, because we need to talk!"

The sudden silence was jarring. The sound of the Beastie Boys ceased instantly, as did Mom's rabid calculator tapping. You could only hear the morning wind rolling in and out of the foyer and a couple of cars driving down Perry Street. Dad's face timidly peeked out from the living room doorway, followed by Kevin's face about a foot below it. Then Mom peeked out from the kitchen.

When Mom saw Merv standing in the foyer, her eyes popped with fear. Then they narrowed into an expression that B.J. couldn't read. Anger? Disgust? Or was it was some kind of mama bear instinct to protect her cub? She turned to Dad and gave him a piercing look—a look that seemed to say that he was the papa bear and that he'd better do something about the lunatic wolf invading their cave.

Dad stepped out of the living room and faced Merv across the long hall. They were locked in some kind of high noon rocker/biker showdown. And then Dad did something that totally shocked B.J. He took off his sunglasses. He pulled them slowly from his face and revealed the gray-green eyes that B.J. almost never saw.

"Hello. Can I help you?" Dad asked, looking innocently at Merv, who was still taking loud, heavy breaths like an asthmatic bull.

Merv raised his stubby, calloused finger and pointed it straight at B.J.'s father. "I *found* you, man. I knew I'd find you."

Dad looked extremely confused. "I'm sorry...do I know you?"

"Oh, don't play with me, Hot Wings," Merv warned. "We don't got time for games, man. He's coming *back*. Six or seven days, maybe less, but he is coming *back* and we need to *move*, man. We need to *mobilize*."

Dad turned to Mom, who gave him her "do something" look.

"Hey, Beej," Mom said with a calm smile. "Why don't you come in here and finish your breakfast, m'kay?"

"Right," B.J. agreed, backing slowly away from Merv toward his mother. "I do have some breakfast to finish."

"And Jayson…" Mom maintained her perfect smile. "Why don't you and this nice man finish your conversation *out*side, m'kay?"

"Well, sure!" Dad agreed, sounding bizarrely like a regular suburban father. "How about it, friend? Why don't we let the kids finish their breakfast, and we'll step outside and talk?"

Merv kept his crazy eyes laser-focused on Dad, not blinking once. "Fine," he agreed. "Outside. But I ain't leavin' till you do what's right, man."

"Well, you betcha!" Dad smiled. "Come on, friend. Let's chat." Dad approached Merv very slowly, put his arm gingerly around his shoulder, and escorted him out to the front stoop, closing the door behind them.

You betcha? This was a seriously messed up situation.

Mom rushed B.J. to the breakfast nook, sat him down, and shoved his chair closer to the table. She poured him a glass of milk, spilling it on all sides of the glass. "You know what, hon? I'm just going to go out there and make sure everything's all right."

B.J. grabbed his mom's arm. "Mom, I don't think you should go out there."

"Oh, don't worry, Beej. He's probably just lost, and he needs some directions."

"Directions to what?"

"You just stay right here."

Mom scampered down the hall and closed the front door behind her. B.J. jumped up from his chair and stared at the door for a few seconds before he realized that Kevin was still frozen in the crouch position by the living room.

"Dude," Kevin uttered slowly. "Who *is* that dude?"

"I don't know," B.J. said, trying to see through the window by the door. "It's Merv."

"Well, who the heck is *Merv*? And what are they talking about out there?"

"I don't *know*," B.J. said. "But we're going to find out."

B.J. grabbed Kevin, and they ran to the foyer. They pressed their ears tightly to the thick cherry wood doors. They could only hear bits and pieces of the conversation, and it was driving B.J. crazy.

Merv growled something that sounded like "The time is *now*. If we don't do this right now, he'll be gone for another *five years*."

But then Mom shushed Merv and everything got quiet again. B.J.'s ear started aching from being pressed so hard against the door.

Mom said something to Merv, but B.J. couldn't make it out. "*What* did she say?" he whispered to Kevin.

"I'm not sure," Kevin whispered. "Something about 'just leaving him alone' or something like that?" Kevin dropped down to his pudgy knees and tried listening through the mail slot instead. B.J. dropped down next to him.

"That was *not* why we came back," Dad said. *Came back from where?* Was B.J. even hearing him right?

Then Merv was going off on another one of his mush-mouthed rants: "And what's right is right!...[*something, something, something*]...if you didn't believe it, then you wouldn't have gone running, Hot Wings!...[*something, something*]...It's called *destiny*, man! One finger, one pinky, man!"

One finger, one pinky? Say *what*? That was obviously not what he'd said.

"Did he say something about Pringles?" Kevin whispered.

"I thought he said 'finger,'" B.J. groaned. "One finger."

"Nah, man, he said 'some Pringles,'" Kevin insisted. "Some Pringles and some Twinkies."

"I thought he said 'one finger, one pinky.'"

"One *pinky*?" Kevin scrunched his face into a disgruntled ball of disbelief. "Why would he be talking about *pinkies*?"

"Well, why would he be talking about *Twinkies*?"

"'Cuz the dude is *hungry*, Beej. That's a good combo. Pringles and Twinkies? Oh man, now I want some Pringles and Twinkies—"

"*Shhhhh!*" B.J. tapped Kevin's head to shut him up. "I think he's leaving."

"What?"

"*Shush* it! I think Merv's going."

B.J. jumped up from the floor and ran to the window that looked out onto Perry Street. Merv was stomping down the front steps in his chunky leather boots, but he was still yelling something back at Mom and Dad.

"Five years!" Merv shouted, pointing his finger squarely at Dad. "This has to happen *now*, Hot Wings! *You* know it, and *I* know it, and everybody else knows it!"

"Well, it was nice meeting you too," Mom called back with a polite smile. "I hope those directions were helpful!"

"You disappoint me, Hot Wings!" Merv shouted with another jab of his finger. "You disappoint *me* and *all* of New Jersey!"

With that, Merv turned away and marched toward his dusty Harley-Davidson, which was precariously parked on the sidewalk. He mumbled angrily to himself as he pulled on his leather gloves and slipped on his wraparound shades. But something made him stop. He whipped his head toward the window, zeroing in on B.J. with a fiery, goggle-eyed stare that could have melted a man's face.

The moment their eyes met, B.J. let out another mini-monkey scream. He couldn't help it. It was just a tiny, one-second scream—more like a high-pitched gasp really—and he backed farther into the shadows of his apartment. But even after Merv turned away, B.J. couldn't stop watching him through the window.

Merv reached into the pocket of his leather jacket like he was making sure something was still in it. Once he was sure it was secured, he climbed onto his bike, kick-started the motor, and revved it up with two deafening twists of the throttle. He gave Dad one last dirty look, pulled away from the sidewalk with a piercing screech, and jetted down the street in seconds flat. But even in that lightning flash of black dust and burning rubber, B.J. saw it happen.

The thing that Merv had secured in his pocket hadn't been very well secured. Just as he pulled away from the sidewalk, the small object slipped from his leather jacket, toppled over the back of his bike, and fell onto the soil by a newly planted tree. B.J. probably would have missed it if he hadn't been watching Merv so closely, but now his eyes were fixed on the mysterious black object lying in the dirt. He had to know what it was, and he had to know immediately.

Mom was already turning the doorknob to come back into the house.

B.J. leaped behind the door, grabbed Kevin's arm, and squeezed it tightly. "Dude. You need to distract my folks for a second."

"Huh?"

"Just tell them I'm still in the kitchen, all right? Two minutes."

"Why?"

"Just *do* it."

Mom and Dad opened the door, and Kevin wasted no time. "Beej is still in the kitchen!" he blurted out. B.J. rolled his eyes.

"Okay," Mom said, looking confused. But her troubled mind was clearly elsewhere, which was good for B.J. Mom and Dad stepped into the foyer, and B.J. slipped around the door just before they turned to close it. As they shut the door behind him, he leaped down the front stoop and crouched down next to the tree. He pulled the slim black object from the soil and dusted it off with his forearm.

It was a weathered black book as slim as a child's picture book and as small as a pocket bible. The front cover was even textured and faded like an old bible, and the title was etched in crumbling gold leaf:

The Legend of the Good Supreme

Under the title was an etched symbol that B.J. had seen a few short minutes ago tattooed on the side of Merv's neck: a pointy-fingered hand making the devil horns.

B.J. suddenly felt a little queasy. He had no idea what to make of the tiny book, but he was certain it was something he was not meant to see. He started to open it, but a deep gut instinct made him stop. He shoved the book into his back pocket before sneaking back inside. He wasn't sure he wanted anyone to see it, including Kevin. B.J. wasn't even sure *he* wanted to know what was inside its tattered pages.

As soon as he got back to his bedroom, he crammed the book into the bottom of his backpack and made a promise to himself: He would not even think about Merv or the book for the rest of the day. There was still a chance that he might have an awesome first day of junior high in New York.

CHAPTER two

It was an absolute nightmare. No, it was worse than a nightmare. The first day of junior high was scary enough, but the first day of junior high in New York? That was a whole other level of terror.

For one thing, B.J.'s new school was called the Log Cabin School. What kind of a name was the Log Cabin School for a junior high? Why wasn't it named after a president or some rich dude like a normal school? He'd pictured all the middle schoolers hopping and skipping to class in big, puffy prairie dresses and rawhide suspenders. But, of course, the reality was far worse. This was Greenwich Village, where everyone was born cool. How was he supposed to fit into their sophisticated world? He didn't have any tattoos, he didn't speak French, and he'd never eaten sushi. Worse than that, he was a foot taller than most kids his age and skinnier than a scarecrow.

Entering the Log Cabin auditorium was more like entering a

posh nightclub than a junior high. All the kids were piling into the theater for some kind of hip New York version of a pep rally to celebrate their first day back. Trying to carve a path through the raucous shoulder-to-shoulder crowd, B.J. felt like a stumbling giraffe, lost in the jungle of cool kids and constricted by a pair of painfully stiff khaki pants.

His dad had bought him some new Skechers and taken him to Abercrombie and Fitch to buy him some new jeans. Dad understood that B.J. only had a couple of things going for him as he entered this bold new world: he had nice purple-blue eyes, and he had a big head of jet-black hair that looked sort of messy-cool when he didn't cut it. But Mom was not a fan of anything that made B.J. look cool. After "The Merv Incident," she'd convinced him to change into a blue button-down shirt, penny loafers, and a pair of wrinkle-proof khaki Dockers.

B.J. had argued his heart out. He'd reminded her that everyone used to call him "Dockers" back in Cleveland. And he did *not* want to be "Dockers" in New York. But she'd still convinced him to wear the khakis, swearing to him that no one would call him "Dockers" anymore.

"Hey, *watch* it, Dockers!" a raspy voice shouted from behind him. "You just kicked Lola in the head, dude!"

Five and a half minutes. That was how long it had taken Manhattan's hipster elite to declare war on B.J.'s pants.

★ ★ ★

He whirled around and found himself face-to-face with a tall Swedish-looking boy who was sporting a spiky blond fauxhawk and a short black leather jacket. He was shooting daggers at B.J. with his ice-blue eyes and holding hands with a beautiful Asian girl in a pink mini-dress. B.J. turned to the girl and began apologizing profusely.

"Oh my God, Lola, I am *so* sorry. I so didn't mean to kick you in the head, I was just—"

"No, she's not Lola," the Viking interrupted. "*She's* Lola." He shoved his scuffed black guitar case into B.J.'s face. "Lola" was written across the case in white, bulky script letters. The rest of the case was covered in grimy old rock band stickers that had either been scratched to shreds or ripped away. The kid looked like he was ready to rip B.J. to shreds too. "You just kicked my sweet Lola in the head, bro. And now I'm angry."

B.J. wasn't sure what to say next. He was all too familiar with the idea of guys naming their guitars. His father had spent most of his Sunday afternoons strumming a powder-blue Fender Stratocaster named Shawna, but this kid seemed to think of his guitar as more than just a friend. "Well, I'm really sorry I kicked your—"

"No, don't apologize to *me*, dude. Apologize to *her*." He pushed the guitar farther into B.J.'s face.

"What do you mean apologize to her? How can I apologize to a—?"

"Hey! Do you want to make this right or not?"

"Of course, I do," B.J. mumbled. He glanced at the guitar case. "I'm, uh...I'm sorry, Lola."

"Oh, come on. Say it like you mean it, bro. Lola can tell when you're lying."

B.J. focused on the top of the guitar case, figuring that was the closet thing to Lola's "face," and he tried to look remorsefully into her "eyes."

"Look, Lola, I'm really sorry, all right? I don't know what happened. It's just so crowded in here, and I'm very tall for my age, and you were so low to the ground that I didn't see you down there, and the next thing I knew—"

"Okay, *stop*." The Asian girl grabbed B.J.'s arm. "That's enough, Jann. He doesn't get your unique sense of humor. Jann's just messing with you, okay? You don't have to apologize to his guitar."

The Viking's lips curled into a nasty little smirk, and B.J. knew it was official. He had just made his first archenemy at the Log Cabin School: a deluded Swedish Guitar Psycho named Jann.

"Hi! I'm Gracie Park—"

But Gracie didn't get to say another word because Jann grabbed her hand and pulled her the rest of the way down the auditorium's aisle.

Okay, I hate this place, B.J. decided. His breaths were growing shallow, and his throat was starting to close up like he had a noose around his neck. What if everyone at this school was as evil as Jann?

Come on, you can handle this, Levine, he told himself. *Do NOT have a Panic Moment.*

That's what Mom called it whenever B.J.'s worries grew so intense that he either had difficulty breathing or the distinct feeling that his head was going to explode. She called it a "Panic Moment" or a "P.M.," as in "calm down, sweetie, you're just having a P.M." Unfortunately, it sounded a lot like the abbreviation for a bowel movement, and on his first day of sleepaway camp, an entire busload of kids thought his mother was saying, "calm down, sweetie, you're just having a B.M." That had taken most of the summer to live down.

Do NOT freak out, Levine. No P.M.s and no B.M.s. Keep on breathing. But he looked up at the auditorium walls, and he was convinced they were closing in on him.

The theater was a cramped little space with a dizzying mix of Greek-style architecture and Arts and Crafts murals painted on every surface. Cheap statues of Plato and Aristotle were glaring at him from either side of the stage while the black-and-white masks of comedy and tragedy stared down at him from the ceiling. *You need to get out of here. Find a place to hide. Run for the hills, Levine!*

He didn't waste another second. He began backing himself down the aisle, searching the theater for glowing red exit signs. He peered over the chattering masses in search of an escape route, and finally, there it was! A narrow spiral staircase next to the stage. It would take a major sprint to scoot past the teachers milling around the podium, but if there was one thing B.J. was good at, it was running. Especially running away.

The spiral staircase led down to a small basement room with a ratty lime-green carpet and some rusty stage lights piled against a red brick wall.

B.J. collapsed against the cool, hard bricks, tossed his bag down next to his feet, and tried to breathe deeply.

His eyes drifted up, and he noticed the words "The Green Room!" spray-painted across the ceiling in green.

Finally free from the Log Cabin hustle and bustle, he began to relax a bit, but when B.J. stretched his legs, his foot kicked something solid in his backpack.

The book.

That freaky black book was still buried at the bottom of his bag—right where he'd left it. He felt another Panic Moment beginning. He tugged the book out, and flashbacks of Merv's gruff voice echoed through his head.

"*You disappoint me, Hot Wings! You disappoint* me *and* all *of New Jersey! (Jersey...Jersey...Jersey...)*"

Who *was* this Merv guy? What did he really want from Dad? And why did his eyes bulge out of his face like someone was inflating a balloon inside his head? And how could *one man* disappoint *all* of New Jersey?

One of the book's pages was slipping out from underneath the cover. Against his better judgment, B.J. flipped it open. It was a decision he immediately regretted when he saw the handwritten message scrawled out on the very first page:

** WARNING! **

This book belongs to MERV and only MERV.

It is the sole property of B.L.A.S.T.

If you are not a member of B.L.A.S.T., then you better close this book RIGHT NOW and WALK AWAY. I am SERIOUS, man. If you do not close this book and walk away, then there is something SERIOUSLY wrong with you because I just warned you to close it and yet you are STILL READING IT. I am TELLING YOU, man. I swear to God, if you do not close this book right now, then I'm going to BRING THE SERIOUS PAIN, MUCHACHO. It is going to rain down on you like a Bergen County blizzard in November, and you will most likely wish that you were never born.

Close it!

Close the book, man!

I SAID, CLOSE THE BOOK!

B.J. slammed the book shut. His heart was pounding like a jackhammer, and his underarms began to sweat.

His fingers hovered over the cover as he considered Merv's warning. He had no idea what a "Bergen County blizzard" was, but it sounded horrible. And B.L.A.S.T., whatever that was, sounded even more horrible.

This wasn't worth the risk. If he tossed the book into the nearest garbage can, he wouldn't have a thing to worry about. That was obviously the wisest choice.

But he flipped the book back open and turned to the next page anyway.

The next page looked like it had been written by some medieval dude with one of those old-fashioned quill pens.

The Legend of the Good Supreme

Prologue

Here within these sacred pages lies the true story of the Good Supreme, one of history's most legendary rockers. For those who would dare to question His power, let there be no doubt:

Yes, He did breathe white-hot Fire at the Gauntlet.

Yes, He did create all-powerful Magic with His Sacred Pinky.

And, yes, He did save our people from the Great Sonic Doom of the '80s with his Sick High-Voltage Rocking.

Of course, many fools have questioned the Good Supreme's power, and they have questioned the power of this book, but they are really, really stupid idiots, for this book contains within it the one and only Way, and it is the Way that you must follow, young Rockling.

Use this book as the map to your greatness. Let the Good Supreme's story be your guide. Live as He lived and retrace His steps exactly. For if you follow in the path of the Good Supreme and do EXACTLY as He did, then you too will become a MASTER IN THE ART OF ROCKING. You will not just master your instrument. You will become a full-on, fire breathing MEGALORD OF RRRRROCK.

But, PREPARE YE, young Rockling. Somewhere in the shadows of the Eastern Coast, you will come upon THE OVERLORD, and he will

What? He will *what*? The rest of the tattered page was gone. B.J.'s mind was spinning with all the possible endings to that sentence.

You will come upon the Overlord, and he will suck out your brain with his pointy rockin' devil fingers. You will come upon the

Overlord, and he will hypnotize you with his furry goat beard and bury you deep in a Bergen County blizzard. You will come upon the Overlord, and he will slice off your head and use it for a game of devil's tetherball!

He slammed the book shut. That was that. He was never going to open it again. Anything involving someone named "the Overlord" should generally be avoided. He held the book between his thumb and index finger like a slab of roadkill and dropped it back into his bag for immediate disposal.

Once he'd imagined this Overlord playing devil's tetherball with his head, another half hour at Log Cabin assembly didn't seem so bad.

He started to climb back up the narrow spiral staircase, but the rumbling stopped him dead in his tracks.

That was the only way to describe it. There was suddenly a heavy rumbling under his feet, vibrating up through his legs all the way to his neck. He had never experienced an earthquake in Cleveland, but this had to be what the tremors felt like: a frightening, king-size pulse, shaking the stairs beneath him like the crushing footsteps of an approaching giant. *Boom... Boom...Boom...*

What is that?

Or maybe the question was, *who* is that?

He looked over his shoulder and realized that the room had a back door in the corner, covered with red and purple psychedelic graffiti. The tremors were coming from just beyond that door.

Oh God, what did you do? What did you just do, Levine?

He'd opened the book. All he'd done was open the book.

BOOM...BOOM...BOOM...

Run, Levine! Run, you idiot!

But he'd waited too long. Two sharp and powerful claws dug deep into his shoulders. He belted out another high-pitched monkey scream.

"AHHHHHHHHHHH!"

But when he looked up, he saw Kevin's face. Kev looked frozen solid—eyes bulging from the sound of B.J.'s ear-splitting girl-screech. He was standing two steps above B.J., clinging to his shoulders. His fingers may have been bony, but they were certainly not claws.

"*Dude*," Kev complained. "What the heck is *wrong* with you?"

"Wha—What happened?" B.J. tried to get his bearings.

"What happened is I finally found you," Kevin said, exasperated. "Why'd you run away, Beej? You're missing the whole thing."

"What whole thing?"

"The show, dude! Come on. We're going to miss it!"

Kevin dragged B.J. up the remaining steps.

* * *

Back in the Log Cabin Theater, cheers had reached a fever pitch. The entire middle school was on its feet, jumping up and down in the aisles, clapping their hands to a chunky techno beat, and chanting in unison.

"CAN-DY! CAN-DY! CAN-DY!"

Candy? What were they talking about? Did Log Cabin just toss out piles of candy to the masses on opening day?

The deafening beat was threatening B.J.'s eardrums with long-term damage. Was this pounding bass drum the demon footsteps he'd heard in the basement? It had to be. "CAN-DY! CAN-DY! CAN-DY!"

A tall African American man stepped to the podium. He was impeccably dressed in a slim, tailored three-piece suit and a striped silver tie, with a pair of nerdy-cool tortoise-shell glasses resting halfway down his nose.

"Greetings, Log Cabiners!" he bellowed. "My name is Principal Terrence J. Power, and I want to talk to y'all about some *things*!"

"WOOOOOO!" the crowd hollered.

B.J. tried to adjust to the idea of a school principal introducing himself over a pumping techno beat.

"I want to talk about setting some *goals*!"

"WOOOOOO!"

"I want to talk about *achieving* them."

"WOOOOOO!"

"I want to talk about looking deep down inside yourself and figuring out what you're meant to *be* in this life! And then I want to talk about *being* it!"

"*WOOOOOOOOOOOOOO!*"

"But *first*, because I made a certain promise to last year's seventh grade class, what I *really* want to talk about is...the *Cotton Candy Twins!*"

"*WOOOOOOOOOOOOOOOOOOOOOOOOOO!*"

The applause swelled to a massive crescendo as the stage curtains spread open. A troop of girls danced their way out onto the stage in a pyramid formation. Right in front were two petite dark-haired girls who looked uncannily alike. B.J.'s eyes popped when he realized that one of those girls was Gracie Park, decked out in her bright pink mini-dress. The girl dancing next to her had to be her twin sister—the only nonidentical thing about them was that she was wearing a neon-blue dress. With the spotlight shining down on them from the balcony, they really did look like two servings of dancing cotton candy.

"Ladies and gentlemen!" the principal hollered. "Boys and girls! Here now to perform their winning song "'Cuz 'Cuz" from last year's Cabin-Palooza Talent Show, please put your hands together for Gracie and Macy Park—aka the Cotton Candy Twiiiiiiiiiins!"

"*WOOOOOOOOOOOOOOOOOOOOO!*"

A slick bassline kicked in as Gracie and Macy took hold of their microphones and began to rap. Actually, it wasn't rapping. It was more like hot girl disco-talking.

GRACIE: *C.C. One on the mic, on the mic*
MACY: *C.C. Two on the mic, on the mic*
GRACIE: *I wear pink (on the mic, on the mic)*
MACY: *And I wear blue (uh-huh—one, two)*
GRACIE: *We dress like candy*
MACY: *That's how we do*
GRACIE: *So don't give us no attitude*
MACY: *Just 'cuz we dress like a baby's room*

The twins began to sing—showcasing their buzzing Britney Spears–like voices:

Lips by MAC and eyes Sephora
Everything in pink and blue
Dress by Sui and BCBG
All our shoes by Jimmy Choo…

The DJ was in the corner, buried under a black military jacket and a wool cap. He mashed in a sample of a marching drum line as the twins locked arms and spun around in some sort of hip-hop do-si-do. When they jumped back to their mics, they started a chant:

GRACIE: *I'm pretty*
MACY: *Yeeeeah*
GRACIE: *I flaunt it*
MACY: *Whaaat*
GRACIE: *I like it*
MACY: *Mmmm*
GRACIE: *DEAL!*
MACY: *Just DEAL!*

They repeated their chant even louder and broke into their chorus:

You can't rag on my outfit, 'cuz
'Cuz girly is as girly does
You can't rag on my outfit, 'cuz
'Cuz girly is as girly does

B.J.'s eyes were super-glued to Gracie's every move. Having met her in the aisle, this was the closest he'd ever come to actually knowing someone famous. And as far as the Log Cabin School was concerned, Gracie Park was clearly famous. He watched her and her sister spin and pop and swoop and pose, and it was just so…It was so…

Awful.

It was awful. He couldn't put his finger on what he hated most about the Cotton Candy Twins. Was it the fact that they dressed like cotton candy? No, it was more likely the fact that they dressed like cotton candy, and also sang about dressing like cotton candy, and also named their band after the fact that they dressed like cotton candy. Still, the crowd was going so utterly berserk for them that B.J. had to be missing something. He obviously knew so little about music that he couldn't recognize real genius when he saw it.

But the twins weren't even the main event.

"People of Log Cabin!" Gracie shouted. "Right about now, I would like you to put your hands together for a good friend of mine, and the *F.I.N.E.-finest* boy in the history of the eighth grade. Would you please welcome Mr. Jann Solo himself. The one and only Jann Törbjörnnsen!"

The girls in the theater rushed the stage like kids chasing the Mister Softee truck on a scorching summer day. B.J. was nearly trampled as the stampede whizzed by him and formed a groupie army at the feet of his new archenemy.

The girls chanted as they gazed up at Jann in awe. "Jann Solo! Jann Solo! Jann Solo!"

It was the most insane display of idol worship B.J. had ever seen. But when Jann took hold of the scuffed black guitar hanging low from his shoulders and began to play, B.J.'s jaw dropped open.

He couldn't even comprehend what Jann was playing at first—it was that good. Jann had painted the name Lola across his guitar in the same script as on his guitar case, and when his fingers danced along her strings, Jann really made Lola sound like a living thing. He had her crying one second and then howling the next, and all of it came in unexpected staccato bursts between the techno beats.

Kevin latched onto B.J.'s arm. "Dude," he marveled. "This kid is unreal."

B.J. couldn't even answer. He was too busy watching Jann enslave his guitar with his masterful fingers. He was still in mild shock when Jann closed out his solo with an epic, piercing bend of his highest string. It was like Lola was reminding the entire student body that she could scream out a higher note than any mere mortal would even dare.

Jann let his head drop as he played his last note, and the bright white spotlight lit up the platinum blond streaks in his golden fauxhawk. The crowd went wild, and the twins threw themselves back to the mic:

You can say our stuff is fluff
You can say our rhymes are weak
But we'll just diss you and dismiss you
In our secret twin speak
Ippa-kaka-rocka-rocka-boom-mama-shocka-shocka

You don't know what we just said
Rrrum-tum-tippy-tum-chippy-chippy-whippy-tum
You don't know what we just said...but it was mean

The crowd exploded with applause, and B.J. felt a deep, throbbing ache in the center of his stomach. He wasn't even sure why. He just knew that he'd been at this school for less than half an hour and was already completely exhausted.

When he finally got home from his first day at the Log Cabin Circus, he limped into the foyer, grabbed a white washcloth from the downstairs bathroom, ran it under some ice-cold water, and laid it across his aching eyes and forehead. Then he blindly found his way up the stairs to his bedroom and collapsed onto his pillow like a rubber-legged marathon runner crossing the finish line. He didn't even bother taking off his loafers.

Mom had gotten out of work early, which didn't help at all. He really needed some alone time right now, but she'd followed him into his bedroom and planted herself at his bedside, refusing to leave until he gave up some information. "Hon? Please talk to me. How was your first day at school?"

"Not good," he croaked, kicking his shoes off with his toes. He pressed the cold compress more firmly against his eyes.

"Why? What happened?"

"I don't even know, Mom. I don't even know what happened. There were just super-cool artsy people everywhere, and this Viking was going to pound me 'cause I wouldn't apologize to his guitar. And then the Cotton Candy Twins were chanting to each other in secret twin speak, and I was in this basement, and I heard..." He shot up from his pillow and grabbed his mom by the shoulders. "Mom, was Merv really just asking for directions or is he in some kind of hard rock, devil-worshipping cult from the '80s called B.L.A.S.T.?"

B.J.'s mom took a long look at her son. "Sweetheart, are you feeling all right?" She pressed her hand to his forehead. "I think you might be having a P.M., honey, and maybe a fever too." Her face was lined with worry as she rummaged through her purse. "Maybe I have some Tylenol in here. Here, take this." As she continued to search her purse, she pulled out a crisp twenty-dollar bill and handed it to B.J.

Whenever B.J. was particularly sad or ill, his mother gave him cash. Dad said it was part of her evil plan to convince him that contrary to popular opinion, money *was* the solution to most of the world's problems. Mom said she was just teaching him how to handle money responsibly so he would one day come to know the joys of accounting. Most of the money was placed in a money market checking account she'd set up for him. She'd given him his own ATM card, but he'd never found the need to use it, what with his intensely boring lifestyle.

"Mom, I don't need money I just had a really hard day, that's all. But thanks." He snagged the cash and stuffed it in his pocket. He wasn't an idiot.

Mom turned to the doorway and screeched for B.J.'s father down in the kitchen. "JAYSOOOOOOOON! Can you come *up* here please and sit with your son! I need to find Tylenol!" She quickly disappeared down the stairs.

B.J. turned to his bedroom window and peered out at the long row of brownstones across the street. Of all the day's events, the one thing that upset him the most was Jann's mind-blowing guitar solo. He couldn't get it out of his head. All those bold, unearthly sounds. All those brilliant plucks and twangs and moans cutting through the auditorium like pure energy. It wasn't just the incredible way Jann had brought his sweet Lola to life or even that electric moment when the crowd erupted and rushed the stage. It was the way Jann carried himself. Even the way he carried Lola. He was meant to play that guitar, and he knew it. He didn't have an ounce of doubt or confusion about it. He wasn't even fifteen years old, and he already knew who he was. B.J. couldn't imagine what that felt like.

Dad was standing in the bedroom doorway, looking annoyed behind his shades. He was barefoot as usual, wearing a pair of faded, ripped jeans and a disintegrating Def Leppard T-shirt, holding his guitar by the neck. "Um…Mom said you were dying?"

"No, I'm not dying, I'm just tired."

"Oh, cool. Well, then I'm just gonna—"

"No, Dad, *wait.*"

Dad was halfway out the door when B.J. managed to call him back in.

"'Sup?" Dad said.

"Could I just talk to you for a second?"

"Um…" Dad peered back down the stairs. "I was kind of having a breakthrough with Dog Wars."

"It'll only take a second, I swear."

Dad scratched the back of his neck. A few more seconds of painful silence, and he finally pulled B.J.'s desk chair over to the bed and propped his feet up, resting his guitar on his lap. He began to strum, but that wasn't going to stop B.J. from asking his questions.

"Dad?"

"Uh-huh, uh-huh…"

"Dad, are you listening?"

"Uh-huh, uh-huh."

"You know, I've got my bar mitzvah coming up in a few months."

"True dat."

"So, I'm basically going to be a man. I mean, like, the Jewish version of a man."

"Okay..."

"So, then, if I'm going to be a man, then, what do you think I'm, like, meant to be in this life?"

Dad breathed out a long sigh. "Dude. You are seriously bumming me with the big questions, Beej."

"Sorry. I just meant—"

"What up, what *uuuuup*!" Kevin suddenly came barreling into B.J.'s bedroom and grabbed Dad's shoulders from behind with a hearty squeeze.

"Kev-*O!*" Dad sang. "*Qué pasa, hombrecito?*"

"Nada, Mr. L. You up for some GH3 before dinnertime?"

"Oh, *hells* yeah," Dad grinned, jumping up from his chair. He turned back to B.J. "You're feeling a little better, right, Beej?"

"Oh yeah, way better," B.J. mumbled.

And just like that, Dad and Kevin were gone. Off to the living room to play another game of Guitar Hero III. Dad on guitar, Kevin on bass, B.J. on nothing.

B.J. sat there quietly on his bed. He felt himself teetering on the verge of a terrible depression, but his eyes drifted toward the backpack lying next to his feet. Yes, he had sworn to throw out the book, but as he watched Dad and Kevin disappear down the stairs like some kind of father and son rock duo, something inside him just snapped. Something in his chest gave way. He sat up and ripped the book out of the bag again, looking for one passage in particular:

Use this book as the map to your greatness. Let the Good Supreme's story be your guide. Live as He lived and retrace His steps exactly. For if you follow in the path of the Good Supreme and do EXACTLY as He did, then you too will become a MASTER IN THE ART OF ROCKING.

B.J. caught a glimpse of himself in the bedroom mirror, and there was a look in his eyes he'd never seen before. It was the same look he'd seen in his dad's eyes whenever he found the perfect lyric for one of his songs. His dad called it "a moment of clarity."

That had to be what B.J. was having right now. A moment of clarity. For the first time in his life, he knew exactly what he had to do.

★ ★ ★

I can't even explain it, Sammy, because it all happened in a split second. I just decided right then and there. I decided to follow the path of the Good Supreme. I decided to live as he lived and retrace his steps exactly. Because even if there was only like a 0.001 percent chance of becoming a Megalord of Rock, that was still a bigger chance than I'd ever had before.

There was just one problem. See, the first few times I'd held the book, I thought it was just really flimsy, but when I flipped through it, I realized it was actually missing a lot of pages. Well, okay, it was kind of missing all its pages, except for six raggedy ones that were barely clinging to the binding. There was that prologue and then there were the title pages for five missing chapters. And the titles of those chapters were really weird. Like, this was the title of Chapter 4:

> Chapter 4
> He embarked on a long and arduous journey to the Holy Land, traveling far from home and enduring many terrifying trials: the Fire Pit, the Rodeo Pig, and, of course, the Overlord.

Say what?

I wasn't sure what to do. How was I supposed to figure out the Good Supreme's entire life story from the titles of five chapters? It was kind of a rough start, Sammy. But every great rocker has to start somewhere.

CHAPTER three

The Legend of the Good Supreme

Chapter 1

He Gathered His Ragtag Band in Only a Week's Time…

At least Chapter 1's title made sense. The Good Supreme had gathered his band in just a week, and that meant that B.J. had to put his band together in a week too. Those were the rules. But there were a few problems right off the bat:

1. He had no idea how to put a band together.
2. He barely knew anyone at the Log Cabin School.
3. Even if he found people to ask, the odds of them saying yes were next to nil.
4. And most importantly, He had no musical talent.

That was kind of a big one. How do you convince someone to join your band when you can't play an instrument and you know next to nothing about music? Based on all the ancient rockumentaries Dad had forced B.J. to watch on the Biography Channel, it seemed like there was only one clear answer: You had to start with your best friend. Dad said at least half the bands in the world had started with two best friends, so B.J. asked Kevin to meet him down in the Green Room before lunch.

"Oh man, what are we doing down *here* again?" Kev complained as he stomped down the narrow spiral staircase into B.J.'s hideaway.

B.J. was more nervous than he thought he'd be. "Well, I just figured it was the best way to..." He was struck silent when he turned around and saw Kevin for the first time this morning.

If you started at his head and scanned down, Kevin appeared to be wearing his standard outfit: a red Puma track jacket zipped up over his sizable belly and a pair of baggy jeans that looked like a denim man diaper. But when you got to Kevin's knees, something went very wrong. Right where his knees were supposed to be, there were now these super-shiny, candy-red, knee-high platform boots. They looked kind of like Superman boots—if Superman had been a chubby, four-foot-tall African American kid with no knees.

"What?" Kevin asked. "What's wrong?"

"Um...the boots...?"

"Oh, these?" Kevin grinned and pointed down at his feet. "These are my Bootsy Boots, baby."

"Your what?"

"My *Bootsy* Boots. You know, like Bootsy Collins?"

"Who's Bootsy Collins? Was he a pirate? Are those pirate boots?'

"No, they're not *pirate* boots. They're *funky* boots. You wouldn't understand."

"I would too! I can be funky."

"Nah, you can smell funky, Beej—that's a totally different thing."

"Just tell me what's up with the boots please."

Kevin cautiously wobbled his way down the rest of the spiral staircase. He was clanking with every step—like the world's clumsiest cyborg. "Look. Think about it, Beej. Nobody knows us here. Nobody knows anything about us. They don't know that you won the Math-Ma-Tazz championship three years running. They don't know what happened to me at the Meatball Massacre of '08. They don't know that everyone called you 'Dockers' or that everyone called me 'Short Round.' Heck, they don't even know we're from Cleveland."

"So?"

"So, this is our *chance*, Beej. This is our chance to reboot." Kev kicked out his giant red boot. "Get it? Reboot? Aw, come *on*, that's good."

B.J. rolled his eyes. "I still don't get it."

"I'm saying we can start *over*. Look, if we were still back home, we couldn't even try to get a new rep till college. But now we get to start from scratch. This is New York City, dude. This is Freak Central. And this time, I'm going to be who I always wanted to be—who I always knew I was for real."

"Who?"

Kevin straightened his posture and cleared his throat like he had a very serious announcement to make. "Beej…I think it's time I told you. My real name is not Kevin Hammond."

"It's not?"

"Not anymore. My real name from now on is KeVonne HaMonde."

"Ke-what Ha-what?"

"Ke*Vonne* Ha*Monde*. You know, 'monde.' That's French for 'world.' I'm KeVonne of the *World*, baby. How cool is that? I thought it up last night with my dad. It's my funk name. From now on, I am KeVonne HaMonde, the Funky Apprentice, and my Funky Master is Bootsy Collins from the greatest funk band of all time: Parliament. And these here are my Bootsy Boots, and I am going to grow into these Bootsy Boots someday, and people will know my *name*. They will *know* KeVonne HaMonde. Do you feel me?"

Anyone else would have been cackling at the sight of Kevin

trying to grow into his giant red Bootsy Boots. But B.J. wasn't laughing at all. In fact, what he felt most was a deep sense of relief. He felt like he had clearly chosen the right best friend back in kindergarten when they had to pick partners to make mini-lasagnas, and he chose the fat kid who looked kind of like Garfield, assuming he'd make the best lasagna. This could not be a coincidence. Kevin was talking about becoming a whole new man in New York, and that's exactly what B.J. was trying to do.

"I *totally* feel you, Kevin."

"Ke*Vonne.*"

"I totally feel you, KeVonne. I want to start from scratch too." His heart began to race because he was about to say it out loud for the very first time. "And that's why…I want you to join my ragtag band."

KeVonne looked confused. "Wait, what's a ragtag band? Is that a math thing?"

"No, it's not a *math* thing. A *band*. I'm starting a band. I'm going to be doing some sick, high-voltage rocking, and I would like you to rock with me. Will you rock with me, KeVonne?"

KeVonne studied B.J.'s face. The laughter began slowly at first. "Huh-huh-huh…" But then it got louder and louder until it just exploded. "*BAAAAAAH*-HAHAHAHAHAHAHA—WHOA!"

KeVonne the Funky Apprentice fell over. His uncontainable laughter and his wobbly boots had ruined his balance, sending him tumbling to the floor in a roly-poly blur of denim and candy red. Now he was writhing around on the lime-green carpet, giggling. "Oh man, that was good, Beej. People always say you're not funny, but you're *funny*, dude! You totally had me—"

"I'm *not* kidding!" B.J. snapped. "Will you be in my band or not?" He swallowed hard, waiting for the next round of thunderous laughter.

KeVonne stared at B.J.'s desperate expression and realized he was dead serious. Then he broke into another smile. Only he wasn't laughing this time. It looked more like a grin of...excitement?

"I *love* it!" Kev squawked. "Oh man, I love it, I love it! Now's the time to start a band. Now's the time to—wait, help me up." He couldn't get back to his feet without a small assist from B.J. "Now's the time to bust onto the Log Cabin music scene for real! I don't want to spend the rest of my life playing Guitar Hero with your pops—I want to be in a *real* band."

"Then let's do it," B.J. said.

"Heck yeah, let's do it!" The two boys bumped fists and slammed into each other for a celebratory hug, which turned into a noble effort to keep Kev from toppling over again. "Okay, so who else is in the band?"

Who *else*? Now he was supposed to have an entire *band* put together? This whole rock and roll lifestyle was moving too fast already. "I—I don't know. I haven't asked anyone else."

"Okay, that's cool. Don't freak out, Beej. Most important, we need an awesome guitar player. You gotta have a totally genius guitar player or the band doesn't stand a chance. And he needs to be, like, a super-stud because every rock band needs at least one super-stud."

B.J. frowned. He knew he wasn't exactly a "*super*-stud," but did Kev really have to rub it in right now? He was trying to step up from "Dockers" status to rock and roll superstar.

"Aw, come on," Kev said. "You're like a solid B, B-plus, Beej. Don't get all insecure. We just need a straight-up A-plus-looking dude. Oh, hold up I've *got* it, I've *got* it. We need that kid."

"What kid?"

"The goldilocks kid from the Cotton Candy Twins. The one with the mad skills. Jann Turbo-Tron. That kid was unreal. *That's* who we need."

"Oh, no way." B.J. waved his hands. "That kid hates my guts. He almost murdered me for kicking Lola."

"Who's Lola?"

"His guitar. She's like the love of his life."

"Oh man, he's crazy too? That's *perfect*. The mad genius guitar player with the mad skills—that's *exactly* what we need. You *gotta* get him, Beej. But there's just one little problem."

"What?"

KeVonne scrunched his face into a tight, wrinkly ball.

"Well...you don't really play an instrument or anything, so what are you going to do in the—?"

"AAAAAAHHHHHH!" B.J. screeched.

"*Yes!*" KeVonne shouted. "That's it! Your psycho-monkey-scream! You've got those *pipes*, dude. You're the lead singer!"

KeVonne thought that B.J.'s scream was an audition for the lead singer position in the band, but it couldn't have been more real. It's just that KeVonne hadn't yet noticed the chalk-white, ghost-faced albino man standing in the darkened doorway of the Green Room.

★ ★ ★

B.J. had never seen an albino in person. He had also never met the Rolling Stones' Keith Richards—he'd only seen him in those rockumentaries on the Biography Channel—but staring at the pasty old ghoul in the doorway, it looked like some mad scientist had spliced the two together into a terrifying genetic hybrid: The albino Keith Richards.

He was silhouetted at the top of the stairs, the pale light of the Green Room reflecting off his craggy, colorless skin, making his face look like crumpled white tissue paper. His hair was bursting out of his blue bandanna in a chaotic mess of white and white-blond. His bandanna seemed out of place with his dark gray blazer and his rumpled gray dress slacks, but then again, his slacks were tucked messily into a pair of dusty gray biker boots, so nothing really fit together.

B.J. was tempted to scream again, but he kept it in check, fearing that Albino Keith might attack if frightened or provoked, like a troubled orangutan.

"Who...Who are you?" B.J. stammered.

KeVonne finally noticed Albino Keith in the doorway, and he recoiled with a spastic shiver.

Albino Keith stepped slowly out of the darkness and raised his skinny powder-white finger. "You ask the wrong question," he proclaimed in a scratchy baritone. "The question is not who am *I*. The question is, what are *you* twos doing down here? You ain't supposed to be down here."

He pointed his long finger at the boys, and B.J. felt a cold chill run through his bones. The way Keith said "you twos" made him sound like mobster-albino Keith Richards, and that was just too many scary things at once.

And then B.J. had a dreadful thought. What if Merv hadn't come to New York alone? What if he'd been riding all those lonesome highways with a deranged, elderly albino sidekick in dress slacks?

Oh God, he's here to take the book back, B.J. realized. *He's here to punish me for my crimes against Merv. I have made a terrible, terrible mistake.*

"I, uh...we..." B.J. tried to force his dry throat to swallow so he could speak, but he was distracted by the sound of his own beating heart. He could feel it trying to pry its way out of his chest as his pulse grew louder inside his head—so loud that it sounded like a bass drum rehearsing for a rock show inside his rib cage—so loud that it sounded like...

Footsteps. That's what it sounded like. Heavy, booming footsteps.

Oh God, it was the *same* sound. The same sound he'd heard the last time he was standing in this abandoned basement.

He slowly backed himself next to KeVonne—keeping his gaze fixed on Keith's pale, cloudy eyes. "KeVonne? Do you hear that sound?"

BOOM...BOOM...BOOM...

"Hear it?" Kev whispered. "I can feel it shaking the whole floor, dude. What *is* that?"

Maybe Albino Keith had not come alone. Maybe he'd brought along a man with bigger feet than Bigfoot. Or maybe it wasn't a man at all. Maybe it was more like...an overlord?

"Kev," B.J. whispered from the corner of his mouth.

"Huh?"

"Run, dude."

"What?"

"RUN!"

B.J. reached back and ripped open the graffitied door as Keith charged down the stairs in his silver-buckled biker boots.

"Hey!" Keith growled. "Where do you twos think you're going?"

"Go, go, go!" Beej shouted, pushing Kev through the doorway.

The booming demon footsteps grew a hundred times louder as Kev and Beej stepped into a maze of basement hallways.

"Which way?" Kev squeaked.

"Just run!" Beej replied, taking off like a rocket.

But KeVonne only made it a step and a half before his Bootsy Boots brought him tumbling to the floor.

"I can't!" Kev cried out. "These ain't running shoes, dude. These boots were made for funk!"

"So take them *off*," Beej ordered, turning back.

Kev rolled onto his back and tugged desperately at his Bootsy Boots, but he couldn't get them to budge. "It took me ten minutes to get these things on! Just *go*, Beej! Go on without me, man."

Albino Keith hurled the graffitied door open, and B.J. ducked around the corner, peering back cautiously to keep his eye on KeVonne.

"Where's the other one?" Keith demanded.

"What other one?" Kev said.

"The other kid. Where'd he go?"

"I don't know who you're talking about, sir," Kev replied. "Who *are* you, dude?"

"I'm the school *security* guard," Keith groaned. "What do I look like?"

"You look like one of those zombies from *The Pirates of the Caribbean*."

"Hey! Mind your manners, Funky Santa! Just tell me which way the scarecrow kid went!"

"I really don't know who you're talking about, sir."

"Forget it! I'll find him myself." Keith stepped coldly over Kev and peered down the hall. He couldn't have cared less about Kevin. B.J. was clearly his only prey.

With Kev safely out of the picture, B.J. skittered down the hallways at breakneck speed, taking the tight corners as best he could in his slippery penny loafers, searching for the way out of this endless basement maze. He could have been running in circles for all he knew. All the wood-paneled doors looked exactly the same. The only things he knew for sure were that Keith was close behind and that those other demon footsteps were getting even closer.

B.J. froze in the middle of the hallway. He'd eluded Keith for a few short seconds, but now he was standing stock-still under the harsh fluorescent lights in shock. He had finally come face-to-face with the marching demon itself.

She couldn't have been more than four-foot-four. Maybe even shorter if she hadn't been sitting on that drum stool. She was wearing a skinny black-and-white T-shirt that said "Pavement" on the front, and her jagged jet-black bangs were falling over her right eye, fluttering up and down every time she pounded her drums. And she was most definitely *pounding* those drums.

B.J. had stumbled to a halt at the wooden door, and now he was peering through the narrow Plexiglas window, watching this little pixie whale away on her sparkly red drum kit as the floor shook beneath his feet.

It was her bass drum. The entire time, that was all it had ever been. She had such a powerful right foot that every kick of her bass drum was echoing through the hallways, rattling the rickety old basement floor like the sound of a stomping demon. B.J. only had a few seconds to process this shocker because Albino Keith was hot on his heels. Barely stopping to think, he kicked open Pixie Girl's practice room door, slammed it behind him, and slid down onto his butt, ducking his head beneath the window to hide.

"Oh, don't even say it," Pixie Girl warned, narrowing her eyes. "No, I will *not* keep it down. This is my room for twenty more minutes, and this is the way I play. I play *loud*. And I will *not* play with the brushes, because I don't play *smooth jazz*!"

"Shhhhhh!" B.J. mashed his fingers to his lips, pleading for her to zip it.

"Ex-*cuse* me? Did you just shush me? Oh no, you do *not* shush a drummer, dude—"

"Shhhhhhh!" B.J. could hear Keith's biker boots turning the corner of the hallway. "Please," he croaked, straining to keep his voice down. "Just for one minute. He's after me." He pointed to the window above his head just as Keith clomped his way up to the door. He shut his eyes and prayed that Keith would jog by, but his boots came to a standstill. B.J. could literally feel Keith standing on the other side of the door.

"Who is that?" Pixie whispered. She stared at Keith through the window.

B.J. placed his finger to his lips one last time and silently begged her to wait through a marathon moment of silence.

And then his prayers were finally answered. Albino Keith caught just enough wind to march on, and he wheezed his way down the hall, continuing his search for "the scarecrow kid."

"Okay, seriously, who was that?" Pixie looked more fascinated than angry at this point.

"I guess he's the school security guard," B.J. replied, wiping the thick beads of sweat from his temples.

"Since when?" she asked.

"I don't know. I've only been here for two days."

"Huh. He must be new. So we have an albino security guard? That is so cool."

"No, not cool. I think he was trying to destroy me. Or at least take me to the principal's office."

"Why?"

"I don't know. He said we weren't supposed to be down here."

"Well, are you a musician?"

Awkward silence suddenly filled the cramped little practice room.

"A what?" B.J. said.

He didn't know why he'd said "a what?" He'd heard her question; he just wasn't anywhere near ready to answer it. Not that he didn't know the answer. The answer was "No, I am not a musician. I am the furthest thing from a musician." But that wasn't going to cut it. Not since he'd made the momentous decision to follow in the path of the Good Supreme.

"Um…yes," he declared. "Yes, I am. I am a musician. Actually, some would say that I'm kind of a master in the art of rocking."

Pixie stared at him. "Like, who would say that?"

"Um, some would say that. I'm B.J." He quickly stepped forward and reached over the drums to shake her hand.

"Layla," she said, "and, yes, I'm named after the Eric Clapton song, but I don't want to talk about it because I *hate* Eric Clapton and every other English guy who plays fake blues guitar."

"Oh, I know," B.J. said. "Clapton—don't even get me started."

"No, go ahead."

B.J. froze. "What?"

"What do you hate about Clapton?"

"What do I hate about…?"

What is this, a quiz? Oh, dude, think, Levine! Who the heck is Eric Clapton? He raced through his fuzzy memories of all the bad rockumentaries. When that didn't work, he tried to picture the covers of his dad's massive CD collection. *Wait. Is Eric Clapton the one with the girly haircut and the beard?*

"Well, first of all," B.J. shrugged his shoulders nonchalantly. "That *beard*…?" He held his breath, waiting for her reaction.

"I *know*." She jumped out from behind the drums. "That stupid beard. *Totally*. What is it with the white blues guys and the beards? Why can't they just get a nice clean shave like John Mayer?"

"I know, right?" It took all the strength he had not to double over with relief. One little lie about being a master in the art of rocking and now he'd signed up for the world's most impossible rock trivia game show.

"Plus, he did that horrible song with Babyface," Layla said. "Ugh, my mom used to sing me that song all the time when I was a baby—you know, about how I'd 'change the world' and I'd be 'the sunlight in her universe' and everything? How *lame* was that song?"

"Oh, the *lamest*," B.J. said. "Babyface. I don't even want to talk about it."

"No, go ahead."

"What?"

"What do you hate about Babyface?"

You did it AGAIN, Levine. Now you're supposed to say something about Babyface. What is wrong with you?

As he racked his brains for something to say about this mysterious "Babyface" person, he started to wonder: Was this how musicians made friends? By talking about the music they hated?

"Well, you know," he mumbled. "Babyface. I mean…the man's got a face like a baby."

Terrible, terrible answer. She could tell he knew nothing about Babyface. He needed something else quick or his cover was blown.

Think of another band you hate before she has a chance to answer. Think of someone you've actually SEEN this time.

"You know who else I hate?" he said.

"Who?"

"I hate the Cotton Candy Twins." He cringed slightly, afraid that he might have just insulted her local Log Cabin heroes. But she didn't look offended at all. In fact, she stepped toward him, leaned forward, and hugged him. She actually hugged him.

"Oh my God, *thank* you," she sighed, as if a huge weight had just been lifted off her shoulders. "I swear, I thought I was the only one."

B.J.'s body went as rigid as a guitar string. Somehow, a girl he'd met less than five minutes ago was giving him a hug. Was this a New York City thing? Could you just hug girls you didn't know if you both hated the same bands? It was an awkward hug, given that his arms had gone numb and she was nearly a foot shorter than he was, but it didn't seem to bother her in the least. Even after she let go, she continued to stand oddly close.

"I can't *stand* the Cotton Candy Twins," she said. "They are the lamest. I couldn't even go to the assembly yesterday because I knew they were going to do that awful song about their outfits, so I came down here to practice. I don't get why everybody loves them so much, do you? It's not music, it's just icky poppy fluffy cheese. You know what I mean? It's like a big bowl of Cheez Whiz. Do you know what I mean?"

B.J. still couldn't get past the hug. His stomach felt like a blender that had been set to gurgle. An embarrassing pink flush had invaded his cheeks. He was trying to think of something to say, but his head felt like it was filled with bow tie pasta and an enormous amount of sauce. So, he simply stated the one and only clear thought in his mind.

"Do you want to be in my band?"

She stared at him like he'd just thrown up on his shirt, which he basically had. He had verbally vomited on his shirt.

"You're in a band?" She stared at his khaki Dockers.

"Oh, I've been in a lot of bands," he lied, "but I'm starting a new project in NYC. I just thought maybe you might want to…" His voice trailed off.

Layla's eyes looked down at the carpet. She took a step back, and crossed her arms over her Pavement T-shirt. All the worst possible body language rolled into one. "Yeah, well, the thing is, I'm, uh…I'm kind of in a few different projects right now, so—"

"Oh, don't even worry about it." He couldn't stand watching her rack her brains for a fake excuse. He dug into his backpack and ripped out a pen and a sheet of notebook paper, jotting down his number. "I haven't even started auditions yet, so here's my number if you want to think about it. Actually, don't even think about it. I'm really just asking anyone who plays an instrument."

Now she looked offended.

"I mean, don't get me *wrong*," he added. "You're awesome. I could hear you playing all the way from the Green Room. I actually thought you were a demon with giant feet."

Now she looked frightened—like she'd just realized she was standing alone in a tiny room with an abnormally tall stranger who was talking about giant demon feet.

"Thanks," she muttered. She snatched her sticks off the snare drum, grabbed his number, and threw her Led Zeppelin messenger bag over her shoulder. "Gosh, I just realized I'm totally late for a class."

"Oh, me too," he said. "Totally late. Late, late, late."

They bumped into each other in an unfortunate game of "Who's going to leave the room first?"

He smiled at her, and she ran like someone had just tossed a flash grenade into the practice room. Then he searched the door for the safest part on which to bang his head in shame.

A demon with giant feet. He'd said those actual words to her. *I thought you were a demon with giant feet.*

CHAPTER four

Jann Solo emerged from the school at exactly 12:05 p.m., just as he had every afternoon for the last three days. He stepped out into the bright yellow sunlight, looking like an anime drawing of a Scandinavian superhero in faded leather and black Doc Martins. Holding Lola firmly in one hand and his overstuffed military duffle in the other, he gazed up at the sun like it was the source of his superpowers.

B.J. had found a stoop across the street from the school where he could duck down and observe Jann without being noticed. It was a filthy little enclosed stairwell beneath a run-down apartment building. Once Jann took off down Bleecker Street, B.J. crept out of his foxhole and followed, making sure to stay a good half block behind him at all times. (He was pretty sure that was the standard spying distance, based on all the movies he'd seen.)

It was true. B.J. had resorted to spying on Jann—maybe even

stalking—but he didn't care because he was running out of time. He was only three days from his one-week deadline, and he'd finally faced facts: KeVonne the Funky Apprentice was right. They needed Jann Solo for the band—there was no other choice. For one thing, he had such a scary amount of talent it could make up for the fact that B.J. had none. Plus, he looked like Thor with short hair, and he came with an instant fan base of crazed, screaming girls. It was a no-brainer. All B.J. had to do was actually talk to the guy. He just hadn't found the courage since the Lola-head-kicking incident.

He followed Jann down Sullivan Street, passing block after block of aromatic falafel shacks, funky vintage clothing stores, French restaurants, Italian restaurants, and cool little coffee houses. Every now and then, there'd be a boarded-up building, covered with black-and-white posters advertising a benefit for the Rock and Roll Hall of Fame: New York (featuring rock and roll icons Daughters of Glenda, whoever they were). B.J. had thought the Rock and Roll Hall of Fame was the one thing that made Cleveland a unique city, but it looked like New York had one of those too. New York seemed to have at least one of everything.

Jann stopped into a pharmacy, and B.J. watched him buy a number of items from the women's makeup aisle, which was a little confusing, but he reminded himself that a lot of rockers wore makeup—especially eyeliner. That, however, was not Jann's last stop. After he left the pharmacy, he trotted down the block and ran into a place called Ming & Ming's Lady Wig Shoppe. That's when things went from confusing to intensely weird. Why did Jann Solo need a lady wig?

With all his weird supplies in tow, Jann trotted across West 4th Street into Washington Square Park, which B.J. recognized by the towering white arch flanked by huge statues of George Washington. The place was literally vibrating with the manic energy of lunching New Yorkers, downtown mommies with their baby carriages, bohemian sketch artists, and guitar-playing hippies.

Jann ducked into a little redbrick restroom on the edge of the park, and B.J. found a new hiding place behind a thick oak tree. He thought Jann was just stopping in for a quick bathroom break, but a few minutes later, a homeless Ronald McDonald came bursting out of the restroom, strumming an acoustic guitar and singing at the top of his lungs, his strawberry-red clown 'fro bobbing in the wind.

Well, I'm Tweetles!
You heard me right, kids!
Tweetles. Gonna rock all night!
I'm the wandering minstrel clown about town
Gonna shake my clown booty and party down! Wooo!

B.J.'s jaw dropped in horror as he hid behind his tree. It was like a bad dream. His guitar idol was crouching down in the chicken-dance position, singing a song and shaking his clown booty for a group of little kids in purple party hats.

"You look stupid, Tweetles!" one of the kids laughed.

"Yeah!" a little blond girl agreed. "Dance, Tweetles, dance!"

Tweetles did as he was told, laying his guitar down on the grass and breaking into a strange Michael Jackson–like pop-and-lock routine. B.J.'s head was spinning

"Okay, *where's* the birthday boy?" Jann shouted in a tragically goofy clown voice.

"Here!" one of the mothers replied. The mothers were all clustered on a park bench behind their kids. The birthday mom ran up and raised her son's hand in the air. "It's Gregory's fifth birthday!"

Jann kneeled down next to Gregory, who had come to his own party fully costumed in a Harry Potter cape, hat, and wand. "Well, hey there, Greg! Happy birthday, buddy."

"I prefer Gregory," the boy said.

"Well, *okay then*, Gregory!" Jann forced out a clown giggle. "Hey, Gregory, do you like *balloon animals*?" He pulled a limp strip of blue rubber out of his pocket, blew it into a tubular balloon in seconds, and began twisting it wildly.

"Yeah!" Gregory said. "Make Optimus Prime!"

"Well, that's not really an animal, now is it, Gregory? How about a wiener dog?"

"Make Shrek!" Gregory ordered.

"Still not an animal, Greg. You don't like wiener dogs?"

"It's Gregory!" the kid snapped. "Sing a song!" he commanded. "SING!"

"Well, okay then!" Jann dropped his half-a-wiener-dog, grabbed his acoustic guitar off the grass, and began to sing to the tune of the Black Eyed Peas.

Well, I got a feeling
That to-DAY is Gregory's birthday
That to-DAY is Gregory's—

"I hate that song!" Gregory barked. "Do Wonder Pets!"

Jann stopped playing his guitar. "What?"

"Do the song from Wonder Pets," Gregory insisted. "*Do* it, clown!"

Jann turned to Gregory's mother, bewildered.

Gregory's mother looked displeased with Tweetles's silence. "He likes the Wonder Pets," she said sternly. "Play him Wonder Pets, Tweetles."

Don't do it, Jann, B.J. pleaded in his mind. *Every boy has his limits. You're Jann Solo. You're an anime guitar hero. You don't do Wonder Pets. Especially not in a clown suit.*

But Jann couldn't hear B.J.'s thoughts. He straightened his

posture, strummed his guitar, and began to sing in a shaky, high-pitched falsetto. He clearly did not know the Wonder Pets theme song, which only made it worse.

Wonder Pets, YEAH
Gregory and the Wonder Pets, YEAH
They're pets…
And they're filled with…wonder…

B.J. dropped his head in his hands. He couldn't look anymore. He just couldn't.

★ ★ ★

B.J. watched as Gregory's mom handed Jann a couple of twenty-dollar bills and then the birthday party moved to the Washington Square Park fountain for soda and ice cream cake. Jann stayed behind and began picking up the abandoned wiener dog balloons from the grass, popping them with his guitar pick and stuffing the rubber remains in his giant clown pocket. Wiener dogs were clearly the only balloon animals he knew how to make.

B.J. knew this wasn't the best time to approach him, but he couldn't stand the sight of a sad, sweaty clown picking up litter in the park like he was on clown probation. He finally stepped out from behind his oak tree, tiptoed over, and began helping Jann pick up some of the tattered balloon pieces.

"Awesome show," he mumbled, keeping his eyes to the ground.

Jann tripped over a tree root and nearly fell on his face. "Wha—what are you *doing* here, Dockers?" he growled.

B.J. was flattered that Jann had remembered his name. "Well, I could ask you the same question, Tweetles."

"Hey!" Jann lunged forward and snatched the front of B.J.'s polo shirt, scrunching the baggy fabric in his powerful fist. "You will *never* call me that name. Do you understand? If you ever call me that name in front of anybody or tell *any*body about this, I will bury you. I will dig a hole in this park, and I will hammer you into it with those loafers, and squirrels will *feast* on your *face*. Do you understand me, Dockers?"

Jann was twice as menacing in clown makeup. His red foam nose jiggled violently with every word.

"I understand," B.J. said, nodding repeatedly. "Message received. But could you maybe take off that wig? Please?"

Jann released him from the insane-clown death grip and shoved him back a few feet. He tugged off his strawberry wig and thrust it into his floppy pocket. Unfortunately, he left the nose on. "How are you even here?" he grumbled. "Why aren't you at school? Wait. Did you *follow* me here?"

"*What?* Noooo," B.J. laughed nervously. "No, I just wanted to ask you a question at school, but you were moving so fast that I never caught up to you, and I just sort of ended up here watching your show, which was really excellent by the way. You totally blew the Wonder Pets out of the water."

Jann snatched B.J.'s crumpled shirt again and hauled off for a punch, but he held back, keeping his fist suspended inches from B.J.'s face. "Listen to me and listen good, all right? There are four words that will never come out of your mouth again. Those words are 'Tweetles,' 'clown,' 'Wonder,' and 'Pets.' If I find out that you have said any of those words, then I will be forced to murder you, and I think we both know that clown murder is the worst kind of murder."

"Yes," B.J. nodded vehemently, feeling an ice-cold chill down his neck. "Yes, it is the worst kind."

"Good," Jann said. "Now get out of here. Go." He shoved him away again.

"Right." B.J. continued backing away slowly. "Can I just ask you one question?"

"NO."

"Right, sorry." He backed up a few more steps. "It's just...if it makes you so embarrassed, then why do you do it?"

"What?" Jann couldn't believe B.J. was still talking, after being given specific instructions to leave. "Why do I do it?"

"Yeah."

Jann puffed out a bitter laugh. "Wait, let me guess. Your dad's, like, some big shot lawyer, right? What is he, a millionaire? Billionaire?"

B.J. laughed. "Oh no. No, definitely not."

"Well, why does anyone do *anything*, Dockers? *Cash money*. You wouldn't understand."

"But what about your guitar playing? You're so good at it, you should be a millionaire by now."

"Oh, you mean from my big record deal?"

"No way! You have a record deal?"

"*No*, I don't have a record deal! What is *wrong* with you, Dockers? Are you always this annoying?"

"Sometimes I ask a lot of questions," B.J. admitted.

"Yeah, well, I ain't got no record deal, and while your mommy's out there buying you blue button-downs, the rest of us need to make some bank, and that's why I Tweetle. It's not like the twins are gonna pay my whole Log Cabin tuition."

"The twins? You mean the Cotton Candy Twins? They *pay* you?"

"Of course they pay me," Jann snorted. "Why else would I play that crap? They just give me the charts and tell me where to solo."

To say that a light bulb lit up over B.J.'s head would be an understatement. It was more like a blindingly white bolt of explosive lightning. It was his second greatest moment of clarity in less than a week.

He dug into his back pocket for his wallet and fished out the completely pristine ATM card his mom had given him to teach him "the joys of accounting"—joys he was only just beginning to understand. He had never once found the need to use the card for himself, but now he raised it up in the air like King Arthur unleashing Excalibur.

"I'll pay you double!" he declared.

"Double what? What are you talking about?"

"What are the twins paying you to play with them?"

"Twenty bucks a rehearsal."

"Well, I'll give you forty to play in my band."

"Your band? What do you mean, like a marching band?"

"*No*, it's not a marching band. It's a *rock* band, okay? And we do sick, high-voltage rocking. Look, what I haven't told you is that I'm pretty much a master of the art of rocking."

Jann had to rip off his clown nose to release the torrents of laughter. "Did you just say you were a *master* of the art of...?"

"Oh, okay," B.J. sighed. "Okay, laugh all you want. Maybe you don't believe I'm a master of the art of rocking, but I'll give you forty bucks to come to my rehearsal and find out."

"There's no way," Jann said. "There's just no way that's happening."

"*Or* I could make an announcement at school tomorrow about

this wacky circus act I just saw in Washington Square Park, featuring the music of the Wonder—"

Jann grappled B.J.'s ruined shirt with both hands this time, staring him down with a long and merciless death glare. "Fifty bucks," he said.

"Forty-five," B.J. countered.

"Done. Now help me pick up these wiener dogs and then we're going to the ATM."

The text popped up at 7:00 p.m., just as dinner was being served.

9175550413: So, are you really a master in the art of rocking?

B.J. hadn't gotten a text from anyone in at least a month. This was a truly momentous occasion. He quickly thrust his phone under the dinner table—just to be sure his parents couldn't see the screen.

BJCell: Who is this? Is this Jann?

9175550413: Jann? You mean Jann Torbjornnsen? Are u friends with him?

BJCell: Kind of. Who is this???

9175550413: It's Layla. You know, the drummer with the giant feet.

B.J. threw his head back and groaned with anguish, startling his mother so terribly that she dropped her carving knife onto the brisket.

BJCell: I DIDN'T mean you had giant feet! I SO swear that was not what I meant. I just meant that when u play, it sounds like a demon coming at you. You know, like, a really, really cool Rock Demon. With really, really hard rocking feet.

9175550413: Well, that's totally what I'm going for. The "Hard Rocking Demon Feet" sound. So, are u still auditioning people for your new project?

His palms got so sweaty that he nearly dropped his phone. What could he say about the totally fake auditions he'd invented?

BJCell: Yeah, had auditions last night. Jann's in, but all the drummers were TERRIBLE. You're a bajillion times better. Do u think u might want to come to our rehearsal tomorrow night?

9175550413: Well, I am kind of in between bands right now. Maybe I could stop by just to check out the vibe.

HOLY MOTHER OF...! Okay, chill, Levine. Chill. Keep it cool. No P.M.s, no B.M.s. No P.M.s, no B.M.s.

She was going to stop by. She was going to stop by to "check out the vibe," whatever that meant.

There was a drummer. He couldn't believe it. There was a drummer, and a guitar player, and a bass player, and...whatever B.J. was. He'd *done* it. He'd gathered his ragtag band in less than a week's time!

BJCell: Yeah, if you want to stop by to check out the vibe, cool. We'll just be chillin.

9175550413: Or we could rehearse at my place if you want? My folks are away at a new age healing and health food convention, so it's just me, my dog Bonzo, and my housekeeper Rosalinda (who totally loves rock). I have a drum kit and some portable amps.

BJCell: Sounds cool, but I think I have a place for us to rehearse.

He shoved the phone in his pocket and tried to mask the insane fireworks going off in his chest. "Hey, Dad?"

Dad was cutting his brisket into tiny pieces. "Uh-huh."

"Do you think I could use the basement tomorrow night? I need to work on a project."

"What, like a science project?" Dad asked with his mouth full.

"Yeah," B.J. replied with a half-smile. "Something like that."

CHAPTER five

The Legend of the Good Supreme

Chapter 2

He watched for the signs and led his band straight to the DOG. He showed the DOG their enormous talents...

Seriously, Sammy. That was the title of Chapter 2. The book said that the Good Supreme got his band together in less than a week, and then the first big thing they did was play for a dog. A dog, Sammy. Like there was this one really important poodle in China who had to listen to me play. It didn't make any sense at all. And it's not like Chapter 3 was any easier to understand.

Chapter 3

Having proven himself to the DOG, he led the band to the Temple of Rock and was shown the way to the Holy Land...

The Temple of Rock? The Holy Land? What?

I told myself not to worry about it yet because I couldn't lead the band to this dog if I didn't have a band to lead. And I couldn't call it a band until we actually played music together. So, I had everyone come over to my house the next day.

When they came over, it was so awesome, Sammy. It totally felt like my band was showing up for a real rehearsal. Mom wasn't home from work yet and Dad was at his new songwriters' workshop uptown.

KeVonne had strapped some American flag swimming goggles over his head to go with his red Bootsy Boots, but no one seemed to think it was weird—probably because they'd all been in bands before. I'd messed up my hair and put on the jeans and Skechers Dad had bought me, and I'd borrowed one of his faded black T-shirts from his dresser that said "Shot Through the Heart'" (no idea, but it sounded kind of badass).

I took everyone down to the basement, where Dad had his shaggy orange rug, a couple of guitar amps, and an old white drum set that he never plays.

I can't even describe what it felt like, Sammy. To be standing there with these guys like I was actually in a band, listening to them all warm up like pros.

Layla started pounding her demon footsteps on the bass drum, staring at the pedal really intensely like she was testing to see how much demon foot it could take. I could tell Jann thought she was too loud because he sort of squinted his eyes and stepped away from the drums, but I think KeVonne was really psyched. He pulled his American flag swimming goggles down over his eyes and nodded his head to the insanely loud beat, plucking out a bass line like he was in a trance.

The whole thing felt totally for real. I felt totally for real. But then everything went super quiet and they all looked up at me.

They were just staring at me, Sammy. Like they were waiting for something—waiting for me to do something. And then I realized, they were waiting for instructions. You know, from the "leader" of the band. They were waiting for the Master of the Art of Rocking.

"So, why don't you play us one of your songs, oh great master?"

Jann bowed sarcastically to B.J. as the basement went eerily silent again. Even the clock seemed to have stopped ticking. B.J. could have sworn he could hear the crickets chirping all the way back in Cleveland. This must have been what floating in deep space sounded like.

Jann and Layla were gazing at him expectantly, waiting to witness a hint of his rock and roll genius, but he'd gone brain dead. It was the Panic Moment to end all Panic Moments. *Do SOMETHING, Levine. Say SOMETHING.*

KeVonne's spunky voice finally cut through the silence. "Hey, why don't we start with that tune we were working on last night, Beej?"

B.J. turned desperately to Kev. "That tune...?"

"*Yeah*," KeVonne replied, with a big nod of his head. "Remember? That awesome tune from last night? The seriously funky one? Let's bust it out!"

"Bust it out?"

"Yes, *Beej*. Don't you remember? You were *improvising* those funky lyrics last night. Remember when you were *improvising*?"

Improvise? That was the secret message Kev was trying to send. He was telling B.J. to make up a song on the spot, as if he could possibly do that. B.J. hadn't even realized he was the lead singer, but then he remembered that KeVonne had already decided for him.

B.J. quickly tried to remind himself of certain facts—facts that his father had shared with him over the years. Like the fact that the Germs and the Sex Pistols didn't know how to play their instruments when they started out (not that he had any clue who they were). Or the fact that Anthony Kiedis had never performed a song in his life when he first jumped onstage with the Red Hot Chili Peppers (at least he'd heard of them). If B.J. truly wanted to become the next Good Supreme, then he'd have to dive into the deep end headfirst—no elbow floaties, no boogie boards, no lifeguard on duty.

"Oh, *that* tune," he finally said. "You mean that funky one we were working on last night!"

"Well, let's hear it," Layla said. "I love me some funk." She raised her sticks high in the air, waiting for her cue to pummel Dad's aging drum skins.

"Oh yes, please." Jann's nasty smirk cropped up in the corner of his mouth. "Please, won't you bring us the funk, Dockers?"

"Oh, he's gonna bring it," KeVonne insisted. "Come on, Beej. Sing 'em that awesome song you wrote!"

KeVonne went into his freaky bass trance and began to hammer out a deep groove. Layla picked up on it immediately and kicked in with her earthquake beat. The snare drum was echoing through the whole basement like a crowbar banging against a giant trash can. Jann stomped down on one of his pedals and started strumming a rhythmic little *wicka-wicka-wicka* thing that was undeniably funky.

And then they all turned to B.J. Waiting for the funk.

He started by nodding his head to the beat. It was all he could think to do. He closed his eyes and tried to look like he was so deep into the groove that there was simply no need to sing. He did that for about two minutes, but then Jann started to look suspicious, so B.J. grabbed the mic, and tried to give them his best soul grunt.

"*Ugh. Mm-hm. Keep it goin' now. Aw, yeeah. Keep it goin' now...*"

"Go awn, now!" Kev hooted. "Bust out the jammy-jams, Beej!"

That was all Kev gave him. "Bust out the jammy-jams." Like that was somehow going to help.

B.J. had run out of options. There was no escape. He could

only tell them to "keep it goin'" so many more times. He had no other choice but to sing, and there was only one thing he could think to sing...

Oh, bust out the jammy-jams
Ugh. Bustin' it
The jams...
Bust it.

It wasn't singing really. It was loud, awkward talking. He tried to add a little hip hop bounce to his step, but it just made him look like a mechanical chicken with a broken leg. He had no idea what else to sing. His mind was spinning at warp speed, scanning the entire cosmos for something else to sing.

Jams. All he could think of were jams.

Ugh. Mama made the jam
Ugh. Put it on the toast
Delicious.

Jann no longer looked suspicious; he looked appalled. His right eyebrow was cocked nearly an inch higher than the left.

KeVonne widened his eyes at B.J. and threw his hand in the air between bass notes. He was signaling for B.J. to take it up a notch—to *pump up the volume.* So, B.J. dug down deep and unleashed his inner funk beast.

Oh, the toast is on FIRE
FIRE TOAST
I CAN'T put on the JAM.

I tried to walk up to the toast with my jar of jam
But it was on FIRE
FIRE TOAST
Ugh. 911 EMERGENCY TOAST
Yes. Hoo hoo HOO hoo hoo
Hoo hoo HOO hoo hoo
911 EMERGENCY TOAST!

"All right. Stop." Jann waved his hands wildly until everyone stopped playing. He ripped his guitar off his neck and scowled at B.J. "911 emergency toast?"

"Yeah," B.J. replied meekly. "You don't like it?"

Jann stepped closer. "Have you ever sung a song before in your life?"

B.J. cackled nervously. "Um, *yeah*. Obviously. Duh."

"Because that's not a song," Jann said. "Hoo-hoo-hoo is not a song."

"Well, I liked it," Layla chimed in, standing up from her drums.

Jann shifted his scowl over to Layla. "Seriously?"

"Yeah," she said, "It's a good story. All this guy wants to do is get some jam on his toast, but he can't 'cause it's on fire. It's sad. It's like a blues song."

"Thanks," B.J. murmured. He smiled at Layla for half a second and then looked down at the shaggy orange rug.

Jann took one more look at each member of the band.

"Well, I'm outta here," he said. He dropped down on one knee, grabbed his box of pedals and cords, shoved them into his duffle, snapped Lola back into her case, and took off up the basement stairs.

B.J. felt a wave of nausea wash over him as he watched Jann stomp away, killing his dreams with every step. It was only when Jann reached the very top step that B.J. realized his mother and father were standing in the basement doorway. He had no idea how long they'd been standing there. Jann muttered an "excuse me" and slid between them, leaving B.J. staring into his father's cold, dead shades in silence.

This was not how he'd imagined this moment. He'd imagined a day, perhaps next week, when his father would hear the sweet sounds of mind-blowing rock wafting up into the kitchen. He'd follow those sounds down to the basement, where he would discover, smiling with sheer wonderment, that the music wasn't coming from the stereo but rather from his very own son.

That was the way he'd imagined it. He had not imagined being caught in the middle of "911 Emergency Toast."

Mom didn't look shocked or angry. What she looked was heartbroken. She was shaking her head slowly, and tears were welling up in her eyes like she'd just received news of a death in the family.

"I'm very sorry, everyone," she announced, wiping the tears from her cheeks. "But I'm going to have to ask you all to leave right now. Everybody please leave. And B.J., I'll need you to join me in your bedroom. *Right now.*"

B.J. squeezed his eyes shut and tried to convince himself that this was not happening.

"No," Mom said. "No, no, no, no."

She was standing next to B.J.'s bed, repeating the word like a broken record. She hadn't stopped shaking her head since coming upstairs, and her arms were still crossed tightly over her chest. "I'm sorry, B.J., but this is not an option."

"Mom, what's the big deal? I can't *believe* you just kicked everybody out." B.J. was slumped at the foot of his bed, grinding his sizable Skechers into the carpet. He could barely deal with the embarrassment of having his mother dismiss the entire band, let alone the deep shame of singing "911 Emergecy Toast" in front of his father and the great Jann Törbjörnnsen.

"I had no choice," Mom said. "I had to stop it. I'm sorry, honey, but this will not be happening."

"We were just busting out some jammy-jams in the basement, Mom. It's not like I'm going on tour or anything."

"Jammy-jams? *Jammy*-jams? Oh God, you're already talking like one of them."

"Mom, calm down, okay? This isn't a big deal."

"Oh, this is a big deal, honey. This is a *very* big deal." Mom dragged B.J.'s desk chair over to the bed and sat at his exact eye level so she could nail him with her penetrating hypno-stare. "B.J., listen to me. This is just how it starts, sweetie. It starts with some innocent jammy-jams in the basement, and the next thing you know, you're forty years old, and you're playing "Don't Worry, Be Happy" for loose change on the subway."

"What? What's 'Don't Worry, Be—'?"

"The *song* doesn't matter, sweetie! B.J., think about your father. Think about his ponytail. That's where this all leads."

"Okay, I won't grow a ponytail. I promise."

"But how can we know that for *sure*?" She popped up from the chair, walked to the doorway, and turned around. "This stops today, honey. Today. Is that understood?"

"But I just wanted to—"

"*Is* that understood?"

B.J. fell back and whacked the bed with his fists. There were a million more arguments to make, but what was the point in trying to argue? He was no match for his mother and he knew it.

"Okay," he muttered to the ceiling.

"I would like to hear you say it."

"Say what?"

"I want you to say 'I will not play any more music. I will not even think about music. Please, honey. For me."

"Mom, don't you think you're being way too—?"

"*Please*, honey. For me."

"Fine." He let out a sigh that lasted as long as he had breath to support it, which was a very long time. "I will not play any more music. I will not even think about music."

"Thank you," she said. "Now, please take off that T-shirt and give it me."

"But it's just a T—"

"Benjamin. The T-shirt." She held out her hand and waited.

"Dude." He tugged the "Shot Through the Heart" T-shirt over his head, handed it to his mother, and collapsed back on the bed.

Mom shut the door behind her, and B.J. rolled onto his stomach, peering out the window again at those tall evergreens on the rooftop across the street.

"I will not play any more music," he grumbled. "I will not even think about music. I will not play any more music. I will not even think about music."

★ ★ ★

All I could think about was music, Sammy. I don't think I'd ever thought about music so much in my life. I jumped out of bed and locked my door and then I plugged my headphones into my computer and Googled "Don't Worry, Be Happy."

And then this amazing thing happened to me. It was like all the terrible feelings swirling around in my stomach suddenly disappeared. I'd planned on being depressed for the next six hours, but I'm telling you, Sammy, when that "Don't Worry, Be Happy" song came through my headphones, I felt like this giant ray of sunshine had come bursting through my window, burning away all my depression and my embarrassment. And it wasn't because the song was telling me not to worry and to be happy. It was because the song was so terrible. I think it might be one of the most annoying songs I've ever heard. This guy just keeps saying "don't worry, be happy, don't worry, be happy" a hundred times.

Sammy, if that's allowed to be a song, then I don't think I was half as bad as I thought in the basement! Is "Don't Worry, Be Happy" really that much better than "911 Emergency Toast"?

So I kept listening to music for the rest of the night, studying up. I Googled "worst songs ever," and I just listened and listened to some of the most terrible songs ever made to try and build up my confidence. I felt a little bit woozy after the combo of "Who Let the Dogs Out" and a song called "We Built This City" by a band called Starship. Not only did that song make my skin itch, but it also made no sense. They kept saying that they built this city on rock and roll, but it was so obviously a made-up city.

All I was really doing was waiting for my folks to go to sleep so I could try to write a song on Dad's upright piano (the piano seemed way easier than the guitar).

I kept checking until the light was finally out under their bedroom door, and then I snuck down to the basement and pulled Dad's rickety piano bench up to the piano. I felt so charged up, Sammy. I felt like I could do anything. I knew that I could write an amazing song if I just put my mind to it.

He sat at the weathered upright piano, both hands spread across the keys, poised to discover his first truly astonishing rock song. It would happen right here and right now, at 11:38 p.m., in the quiet confines of a dark and chilly basement beneath the world-famous streets of New York City. He had never once played the piano, but that didn't seem to matter right now. It would just come to him. There were at least ten songs inside his head that were better than "Who Let the Dogs Out." They were hovering just beneath the surface; all he had to do was coax them out and channel them into Dad's piano. He cleared his mind and tried to let his fingers think for themselves.

He figured it was best to start with the white keys and work his way up to the black keys later. Then he decided to start with just one hand, as using both hands required way too much coordination. Using the whole hand still felt a little overwhelming, so he decided to start with one finger. The index finger.

He pressed down on one of the keys and began to play.

Plunk plunk plunk plunk plunk plunk...

Okay, I like it, he thought to himself, but he knew he needed more notes. He shifted his index finger to a second note that seemed to go well with the first and then he added a third note. But then he got lost when he tried to add a fourth note with his pinky. He decided to start again with the first note.

Plunk plunk plunk plunk plunk plunk...

Okay, sounding pretty tasty. When he was good and ready, he switched to his second note and then his third, but then came that pesky fourth note again, followed by extreme confusion.

The problem was becoming clear. He could only play three notes. It seemed like after the first three notes, a song took on a whole other level of complexity that was just way over his head.

But he hadn't tried singing yet. Maybe if he sang while he

played, then the whole thing would start to come together into a fully realized song. So he began his plunking again, cycling through the three notes repeatedly as he cleared his mind and waited for the melody to come to him.

Plunk plunk plunk plunk plunk plunk…

What are the words? he asked himself. *What are the words that come to your mind when you play these three notes?* He reached down into the deep inner core of his untapped creative genius. He let go of all his earthly worries and concerns and sang out the truest words that came to his mind.

I can only play three notes
I can only play three notes
I can only play three notes.

He slammed the piano shut.

Sammy, songwriting is impossible. I mean, it's literally impossible. It's the hardest thing I've ever tried to do, and that's including the Math-Ma-Tazz championships. I have to give it up to the Baha Men and the Starship guys and even the weird "Don't Worry, Be Happy" dude because no matter how terrible their songs are, they're still, like, complete songs with lyrics and a melody and a beginning and a middle and an end, and I have NO idea how they did that. I mean, I know "woof, woof, woof, woof, woof" might not count as lyrics, but compared to a song with three notes, the Baha Men are geniuses.

I must have sat on my dad's old piano bench for another half hour, feeling sorry for myself. How was I *supposed* to become the next Good Supreme if I couldn't write one song?

I finally got up and started moping around the basement because Dad never lets me hang out down there alone. I figured this was my best chance to snoop around.

I started at his computer desk, but that was covered with too many guitar gadgets and harmonicas. I knew he would notice if even one guitar pick was out of place. I turned to his giant wall of CDs, but that just made me think of the millions of songs that all those rock stars had already written. I mean, Mr. Bon Jovi, the grand master of face-rocking, had eleven CDs, Sammy. Eleven. I know because Dad had them all lined up in a special cabinet at the center of his wall. And Bruce Springsteen had sixteen CDs, not even counting the live concerts. I know because Dad had them all lined up next to the Bon Jovis. The first Bruce Springsteen album was called Greetings from Asbury Park, N.J. I pulled it out for a closer look, and that's when I found it.

Now, Sammy, this is the part where I tell you something that I should have told you the second I met you, but I just couldn't. So if you decide you hate me, I totally understand.

I found this dusty old manila folder stuffed in the back of the shelf, behind the Springsteen CD. I think Dad was trying to hide it from me and Mom. All it said on the front was "Atlantic City," which, I'm sure you know, is a city in New Jersey (the one with all the casinos). I thought I might find some old pictures inside, but the only thing in the folder was a gold CD and a piece of handwritten sheet music with Dad's name on top. "Atlantic City by J. Levine," it said. It was one of my dad's old songs. Yes, you read right, Sammy. "Atlantic City" is one of my Dad's old songs.

I plugged the headphones into his stereo and started to listen. Dad's voice sounded way younger. I don't know when he'd made the recording, but it was definitely an old one and oh man, did it rock, which, I guess, you already know.

All I can say is, I was dancing around the basement, listening to my dad sing his song, looking at the top of the sheet music where he'd written his name, and it just hit me.

"Atlantic City by J. Levine," it said.

All I had to do was take a black pen from his desk and write in one little "B" next to the "J." And there it was. "Atlantic City by B.J. Levine."

I know how wrong it was, Sammy. I do. But you've got to understand. I needed a good song. It was the only way, Sammy.

"Hello?"

"Oh, uh…" B.J. stammered and nearly dropped the piece of paper with Layla's cell phone number. She wasn't supposed to pick up her cell at 12:30 in the morning! She was supposed to be asleep so he could leave her a long voice mail message with his bold new lie. Now he'd crash-landed in the middle of their very first phone call. "Layla?"

"Oh my God. *Levine?*"

He was surprised she hadn't rejected the call. He was surprised she was even speaking to him after being kicked to the curb by his mother, but she actually sounded kind of happy to hear from him.

"Yeah, it's Levine," he said. It felt strange when she called him "Levine." "I'm really sorry, Layla. Did I wake you?"

"No, why? What time is it?"

"It's twelve-thirty."

"*What? God.* Rosalinda never tells me when to go to bed. I don't even know what time it is when my parents are away. I guess that's why I never know what time it is. Are you still in New York?"

What a weird question. "Uh, yeah. Why?"

"I just thought your mom might have sent you to military school or something. She looked *so* un-psyched to see you rocking out. Like, weirdly un-psyched, Levine."

"Yeah, I know. My mom's got issues. But wait. Was I really

rocking out?" He shut his eyes the moment he'd said it. He couldn't believe the stuff that came out of his mouth when he talked to Layla.

"Sort of," she said. "I especially liked that 'hoo-hoo-hoo' part of '911 Emergency Toast.' I don't care what Jann says. I think nonsense lyrics make some of the best rock songs. I actually made you a mix of nothing but awesome rock songs with nonsense titles. 'Da Da Da' by Trio and 'Bawitdaba' by Kid Rock and..."

"You made me a mix?"

The line went silent. B.J. thought the call might have dropped until Layla finally spoke. "Yeah, well, it was no big deal. Me and my dog Bonzo were just sitting here watching infomercials and eating s'mores."

"No, I meant...I mean, thanks." *Ugh, just get to the point, Levine.* "Hey, Layla, what are you doing tomorrow after school?"

"Why? You want to come over? I can't meet till six, but then you could come over and I could play you the songs. Maybe we could try to work on that 'hoo-hoo-hoo' part together and see if we can—"

"Actually, I was hoping the band could come over and rehearse?"

Silence on the line again. "Oh, the band. Right. Yeah, totally."

"I mean, we don't have to," he said. "It's just that you said you had a drum set and amps..."

"No, we can definitely rehearse here. But didn't Jann kind of quit the band?"

"Well, I think I can talk him back in."

"How?"

"How?"

He'd prepared this entire speech for her voicemail, but saying it in person was a very different story. Now his brain felt like a giant salad spinner, jumbling all the words together into a blur of wet lettuce. But he had to try. It was the only way he'd become a better liar: practice, practice, practice.

"Well, the thing is, Layla, I really write all my best stuff late at night. I mean, the nighttime is when I really get my groove on, you know?" *Your groove? Seriously?* "Um, all I'm trying to say is, I think I might have just written my best song in years."

"In years?" Layla giggled. "When did you write your first song?"

"Oh, I been dropping bombs since I was like...nine." He slapped his hand over his forehead. *Dropping bombs? Are you even using that right?* "Anyway, I really think this could be the one that takes us to the top. We just can't play it at my house, like, ever, you know, because my mom's so psycho. But I know once Jann hears it, he'll come back to the band."

"It's that good, huh?"

"Yeah," he said. "That good. Also, I'm going to give him eighty dollars."

CHAPTER SIX

"Sweet! You're the first one here! Come in. Come, come, come!"

Layla grabbed B.J.'s wrist and tugged him through the front door of her cluttered loft apartment on East 7th Street. When he stepped inside, he could feel the whole place vibrating with Layla's souped-up energy. Everything seemed a little larger than life. The ceilings were high and the windows were wide, with long straw blinds rolled all the way up, revealing a sprawling view of downtown Manhattan. The setting sun was blasting through the windows, casting a dusty golden light on Layla's canary-yellow David Bowie T-shirt and dark blue skinny jeans.

B.J. didn't feel too out of place, thanks to his Superman-style quick change. He'd left his apartment in the blue button-down and Dockers (telling his mom that he and Kev were going to study for a math test at a new friend's house), but then he'd ducked into the bathroom of the Two Boots pizza place down the block and changed into his jeans, sneakers, and a black T-shirt he'd swiped from his dad's dresser that said, "We're Halfway There..." (no idea, but it was the only clean black T-shirt in the drawer).

Layla's room was exactly what he'd expected: a rock and roll disaster area. The shiny wood floor was littered with CDs, drumsticks, and fuzzy, mangled dog toys. There was a black drum set in the corner of the room and two small amps buried under stacks of jeans. The walls were covered with band posters, but B.J. didn't recognize any of the bands.

"Quick, quick, quick." Layla pulled him down to the floor next to her laptop. "I want to play you these songs before everybody gets here. The 'hoo-hoo' part in "911 Emergency Toast" made me think of these. I think they'll totally inspire you. There are *so* many awesome songs in this playlist. 'De Do Do Do, De Da Da Da' by the Police, 'Mmm Mmm Mmm Mmm' by Crash Test Dummies..."

B.J. tried to pay attention to her playlist, but the only song on his mind was "Atlantic City by B.J. Levine." He'd been running the chorus through his head on endless repeat since the night before...

She took the money all night
She took the money all right
She took the money from my pocket and she turned out the light
She left my blood on the road

She took the love of my life
She took the money, yeah, all night…

Dad's lyrics left B.J. with a million more questions. Why had he been hiding the song in the basement? Had this casino robbery really happened or was he just making up a story? And if it was a true story, since when was money "the love of Dad's life?"

Layla was still chattering breathlessly about her mix. "It's got 'Na Na Na' by My Chemical Romance, 'Lula Lula Lula' by the D.O.G., 'Shoop' by Salt-N-Pepa—"

"Wait. What did you just say?" All the hairs on B.J.'s neck stood up. He darted his eyes down at Layla's computer screen.

"What?" Layla asked. "'Shoop' by Salt-N-Pepa?"

"No, before that. What did you say before that?"

"'Lula Lula Lula' by the D.O.G.?"

The two words socked him right in the solar plexus.

"What's…the dog?" He nearly choked on the words.

"Not what," Layla laughed. "*Who.* The Daughters of Glenda. Everyone calls them 'the D.O.G.' for short. You don't know the Daughters of Glenda?" She pointed up at one of her dustiest posters near the ceiling. Three young blond girls with choppy '80s haircuts, wearing shiny black jumpsuits, leaned against each other like Charlie's Angels, snarling at the camera. "Beware of D.O.G.," it said in the classic block letters of a warning sign.

"Lil' Bow Wow totally stole that title," Layla said. "*How* can you not know the D.O.G., Levine? Haven't you seen all those posters for their big concert on the street? There are, like, five signs on every block."

"*Signs*," B.J. breathed. "Oh my God, the signs..." His heart began to beat too quickly. "Layla, can I use your bathroom?"

"Sure." She noticed his extreme shortness of breath. "Are you okay, Levine?"

"Uh-huh, uh-huh," he muttered, sounding eerily like his father.

He snatched up his backpack from the floor and rushed into Layla's tiny bathroom, shutting the door behind him and locking it. He nearly fell through the pink Hello Kitty shower curtain as he unzipped his bag and pulled out *The Legend of the Good Supreme*, flipping quickly to Chapter 2's title. He'd gone through it a hundred times before, but for the first time, it didn't read like an impossible riddle.

> He watched for the signs and led his band straight to the DOG.
>
> He showed the DOG their enormous talents...

The signs. The signs like the *posters* all over town. He'd seen the posters when he was following Jann. He just hadn't been *watching* for them.

The DOG wasn't some magical poodle in China. It was the initials for a *band*. The Daughters of Glenda. It had to be. This must have been how it happened back in the '80s. The Good Supreme must have seen the signs for a D.O.G. concert and gone right into the club to play for them. The Daughters of Glenda must have *discovered* the Good Supreme's band.

And now they needed to discover B.J.'s.

"Layla!" he called through the bathroom door. "When is the D.O.G. playing that benefit concert?"

"At 7:30 at the Fillmore," she called back. "Why?"

"*Tonight?*"

"Yeah, but there's no way you can get tickets. It's been sold out for months, and they're only in town for one night. I read there's going to be a huge after-party at the Rock and Roll Hall of Fame. You know, totally exclusive. For celebs only."

The shrill ring of Layla's doorbell shook B.J. so badly that he dropped the book into the toilet.

"That must be the guys," she said, running from the room.

The Rock and Roll Hall of Fame. The Rock and Roll Hall of Fame, Levine. Do the math...

Still barricaded in Layla's bathroom, B.J. fished the book out of the toilet and flipped to the next wet page of the book, staring intensely at Chapter 3's title:

Having proven himself to the DOG, he led the band to the Temple of Rock and was shown the way to the Holy Land...

The Temple of Rock. It makes perfect sense! It fits. What is a temple? It's a place where people go to worship. And where do people worship rock? The Rock and Roll Hall of Fame! The Hall of Fame IS the Temple of Rock.

That's where he needed to go. That's where he needed to lead them. He was sure of it. It was more than a moment of clarity. It was an out-and-out revelation.

"All right, I'm here!" Jann's obnoxious voice echoed off Layla's high ceilings as he stomped into her bedroom. "I showed up, Dockers, so where's my eighty bucks?"

B.J. stuffed the book back in his bag and pulled out the photocopied sheet music he'd made for rehearsal. He knew Jann and Kev could read enough music to learn "Atlantic City."

He hurled open the bathroom door like a boy possessed—like a man on a mission. Which he was.

"You get your eighty bucks at the end of rehearsal," he said, slapping a copy of "Atlantic City" into Jann and KeVonne's hands. "But first, we're going to learn my new song. We're going to rehearse it again and again and again till it sounds insanely awesome. Because we have a gig tonight."

He'd shocked the entire band into silence.

"A gig?" Layla sounded terrified. "We've only played together once, Levine. For ten minutes."

"Yeah, what do you mean a gig?" Jann said. "A gig where?"

"It's a surprise," B.J. said.

"A surprise?" Jann snorted. "That's a joke, right?"

"You wrote a new song?" KeVonne looked sincerely impressed as he flipped through the sheet music for "Atlantic City." He looked more than impressed. He looked proud of his best friend. "Dude, I *knew* you had it in you, Beej. I knew it."

B.J. couldn't look Kev in the eye. And not because he was wearing American flag swimming goggles and a red, junior-size paratrooper jumpsuit covered in numerous unnecessary zippers that made him look like a mini-Ghostbuster.

"I think I'm gonna pass on the gig," Jann said, tossing the sheet music back to B.J. "I don't like surprises."

"Oh really?" B.J. said. "I thought you were pretty good with surprises...Tweetles."

Jann's eyes grew dark with rage. His sudden death glare sent a quick shiver down B.J.'s spine, but he had no choice. If the eighty bucks wasn't going to keep Jann in line, then he had to play the Tweetles card. There just wasn't any more time for games.

"Tweetles?" Kev giggled. "Who the heck is Tweetles?"

"*No* one," Jann snapped. "Just give me the music, Dockers." He swiped the pages back out of B.J.'s hands and flipped through them angrily. "What is this? You wrote this song?"

"I just wrote it last night," B.J. said. "See, the nighttime is when I really get my groove—"

"You didn't write this song," Jann interrupted. "When have you ever been to Atlantic City?"

B.J. swallowed all his nervousness, straightened his posture, and returned Jann's angry gaze with a dead-serious look of his own. "Well, there's a lot you don't know about me, Jann."

"Oh really?" Jann said sarcastically.

"Really," B.J. replied. "I have a very complicated past, dude."

He'd said it just to get Jann off his back. He had no idea how true it would turn out to be.

Mom's first text came at 8:30 p.m.

MomCell: Benjamin, it's Friday night. You're supposed to be home for Shabbat dinner. Aren't you and Kevin done studying for the math test yet? Please have your friend's parents send you home in a taxi.

BJCell: But they've invited us for dinner! I don't want to be rude! They can get us a taxi after. Cool?

MomCell: Not cool. I want you back here in a taxi BEFORE 9:30. Understood?

BJCell: No prob.

B.J. quickly silenced his phone and tried to block out all thoughts of his dear mother.

His band had been trekking for blocks now, lugging their equipment through the crowded downtown city streets. All the brilliant white streetlights were glowing like UFOs under the black Manhattan sky.

They'd rehearsed "Atlantic City" for over two hours, but night had come too quickly. Now the pressure was on B.J. to get them to the Daughters of Glenda show before the concert let out and the D.O.G sped off in some stretch SUV limo, never to be seen again.

He still couldn't tell what the band thought of "Atlantic City" or his singing, but he knew that Jann hadn't bailed on him yet, and that had to count for something.

He raced a few steps ahead of the crew, trying to sneak peeks at his cell phone's navigation to find "the Fillmore Theater at Irving Plaza." All he'd told the band was that their gig was "near Irving Place." Layla had asked if there would be a drum kit at the venue, and he'd answered yes just to keep her from asking any more questions. He was basically making up the entire plan as he went along. He hated having to be so mysterious, but he was pretty sure that saying "a man with a goat-fur beard left me this rock and roll bible that says I can become a fire-breathing Megalord of

Rock if we play for the D.O.G." was not the best idea. He didn't want to be hauled off to the loony bin before he even sang a note.

The walk across 14th Street had been intimidating enough. It was B.J.'s first unchaperoned walk through New York at night, and he'd seen his share of weirdness, including two tall men dressed as Cher and Lady Gaga. But it wasn't until they turned the corner of East 15th Street that B.J. truly understood the meaning of New York mayhem.

The entire block between 15th and 16th Streets had been transformed into a human dog kennel. Throngs of wild D.O.G. fans were swarming the bright red Irving Plaza marquee, barking at the doorman.

"*Arfarfarfarf! Woofwoofwoofwoof!*" It seemed to be the "thing" that D.O.G. fans did with each other. B.J. wondered if they even knew they were all just singing "Who Let the Dogs Out."

"All right, what's going on?" Jann dropped Layla's travel amp on the sidewalk and stepped toe-to-toe with B.J. "This is not a *gig*, Dockers. This is a Daughters of Glenda concert, and it's already over."

"I know," B.J. said, craning his neck to get the lay of the land. "We just need to find the stage door."

"The stage door?" Layla's eyes lit up. "I know where it is. I've waited there for autographs. Oh my God, do you have backstage passes?"

"Sort of," B.J. said.

"*Sort* of?" Jann's frustration had been slowly building over the course of their walk. "What do you mean sort of?"

"Layla, just get us to the stage door," B.J. said. "I'll take it from there."

They shoved their way through the barking masses, shouting "excuse me" and "coming through" until Layla had successfully gotten them to a crowded alley around the corner. When B.J. saw the sign for the stage door, he leaned close to Layla and whispered in her ear. "What are their last names?"

"Who?" she whispered.

"The Daughters of Glenda. Give me one of their last names. Who's the lead singer?"

"McSorley. Christina McSorley. Why?"

B.J. stomped up to the stage door and pounded on it good and loud.

Here goes nothing. No P.M.s, no B.M.s. No P.M.s, no B.M.s…

When the door swung open, he had to stifle his scream. The hulking doorman had a shaved head that was completely covered with a spiral tattoo of a black King Cobra. A host of other tats and piercings adorned his arms and face, including six silver hoops along his eyebrows that made him look like a big slab of human fishing tackle.

"*What do you want?*" Snake Head snarled.

B.J. was dying inside, but he looked straight into Snake Head's black eyes and puffed out his chest as far as it would go. "'Sup, homes. I'm B.J. McSorley, and this is my band."

"So?"

"So?" B.J. stared back at Snake Head with wild-eyed indignation. When facing down a 300-pound bouncer, he thought it best to look mildly insane. "*So*, I'm supposed to meet my *mom* inside. Christina *McSorley*? Hel-*lo?*" He made sure not to look at any of his bandmates. If he even glimpsed their shocked expressions, he'd lose his nerve.

Snake Head leaned in for a better look at B.J.'s face. "You don't look like a McSorley, dude."

"Yeah, well, my dad's very Jewish."

"Then how come your last name's McSor—?"

"It's my *stage name*, muchacho!" Seismic tremors were running through his wiry legs, which were surely going to buckle at any moment. "Look, my mom is in there waiting for me and my band. We were supposed to meet her backstage after the show." He thrust his cell phone in the air. "You want me to call her and tell her that Snake Head the doorman is giving us a hard time? Because I am *telling* you, man, if you do not let us in right now, then my mom is going to bring the *serious* pain, muchacho. It is going to rain down on you like a Bergen County blizzard in November, and you will most likely wish that you had never been born, muchacho!"

"Dude, why do you keep calling me 'muchacho'?" Snake Head growled. "My name's *Warren.*"

"Why? *Why?*" B.J.'s tongue was completely numb. "Because that's how I *do*, bro. That's-tha-tha-that's my *thing.* I call people 'muchacho'!" He was breathing so hard, he was pretty sure he was about to puke in Warren's face.

Warren stared at him for what felt like hours. "Fine. Wait here." He slammed the stage door shut, and B.J. collapsed on the grimy stoop, leaning his elbows on his knees. He could feel his bandmates staring down at him. He'd left them all momentarily speechless.

"Okay, I think I get it now," Jann said. "You're just full-on nuts, Dockers."

"I'm not," B.J. mumbled. "We just need to get in there so we can play for the D.O.G."

"*Play* for the D.O.G.?" Jann threw up his arms in disbelief. "Is that the plan, *McSorley*? You can't just knock on a stage door, walk up to some famous chick, and play her a song! That's not a gig."

"Okay, so it's more like an audition," B.J. said.

"No, it's more like psycho!"

B.J. jumped back to his feet. "Well, psycho or not, the lead singer of the Daughters of Glenda is about to open this door, and we're going to show her our enormous talents, all right?"

"Our enormous talents?" Jann turned to the other bandmates. "Does anybody know what's *wrong* with this kid?"

The stage door swung open again, and B.J. readied a huge smile for his new "mother," Ms. McSorley. What he got instead was an entourage the size of Texas, stampeding through the stage door to a rousing chorus of cheers, arfs, and woofs.

"Ms. McSorley!" he called out. "Ms. McSorley, I just need a moment of your time please!"

"Dude, quit it!" Jann grabbed B.J.'s arm and yanked him backward. "You're embarrassing us."

"No, you don't understand," B.J. said. "We have to do this. They're only in town for one night—this is our only chance to play for them, and we *have* to play for them."

"Play for them *where*? In the middle of an alley? You're a stone-cold freak, Dockers. I'm going home."

Layla's eyes were brimming with disappointment. She'd actually believed B.J. when he said they had a gig. "Yeah, Levine. Can we just go home now?"

"And get a ham sandwich?" KeVonne added.

"No," B.J. said. "No, this has to happen *now.* Just follow me and bring the amps." He broke free of Jann's grip and chased after the entourage again, trying to elbow his way through the swirling vortex of muscle dudes, skinny chicks with iPhones, guys with cool glasses, and girls with leather pants and black feathered coats.

"Ms. McSorley! Daughters of Glenda! Woof, woof, woof! Please. This is *really* important." But no one was listening.

When Jann grabbed B.J.'s arm again, his shoulders slumped forward, and he finally gave up. They were right. It was time to go home.

Only Jann hadn't grabbed his arm. When B.J. turned around, he was staring at a large crumpled ball of white tissue paper, which he soon realized was not a crumpled ball of white tissue paper at all. It was Albino Keith's face.

"AAAAAAAAAAAAAHHHHHH!"

The piercing scream rang through the alley like the strangled cry of an opera-singing cat in heat. It echoed in all directions, bringing the crowd to a total standstill. All eyes turned to B.J. and the decrepit albino man grasping his arm.

B.J. hadn't seen Albino Keith since their encounter in the school basement. Now Keith had changed out of his dark gray school suit and slipped on a leather biker jacket with leather pants, but he still had the blue bandanna wrapped around his ghostly white tufts of hair. The question was: what on Earth was he *doing* here?

Slowly, amid the sudden stillness and silence, the D.O.G.'s entourage began to part like a red sea of rocker wannabes. Three blond women in tight black jumpsuits and black feathered coats emerged from the center. One of them stepped ahead of the others, and B.J. was sure it was Christina McSorley, the lead singer.

She was definitely old but remarkably well preserved, with tan, freckled skin, a little button nose, and hair pulled back in a long ponytail that jutted out from the top of her head. Her neck was covered in a ring of tattoos that made her look like some kind of tribal princess.

"Okay, who just made that sound?" she asked. "And why is Albino Keith Richards strangling this kid's arm?"

B.J. nearly fell backward. He couldn't believe mega-star Christina McSorley had confirmed his Keith Richards call.

"I am *not* Keith," Keith complained in his heavy accent. "I am *Paulie*."

Ms. McSorley narrowed her eyes. "Well, is this kid your grandson, Paulie?"

"No, ma'am."

"Then why are you squeezing his arm like an angry grandpa? Let. Go."

Paulie released B.J.'s arm to a host of disapproving murmurs from the crowd.

"I apologize, Ms. McSawley," Paulie said, "but I do security here for the Fillmore, and I think you should be aware that these kids here are *way* underage. "

B.J. was totally lost. Did Albino Paulie do security for the Log Cabin School or the Fillmore New York? Or both?

Ms. McSorley turned to B.J. "What's your name, kid?"

"B.J.," he replied, nervously.

"Have you and your friends been drinking alcohol, B.J.? Breaking any laws?"

"No, ma'am."

"And are you the one who just made that prehistoric screech?" she asked.

"Yes, ma'am," he mumbled.

"Very cool. You've got some serious pipes, kid. I think that was a perfect G-sharp you just screeched."

"Really? Um…thank you?"

"You bet."

The next thing B.J. knew, Ms. McSorley's entourage was closing back around her like a bear claw. She was turning to leave, and B.J. could not let that happen. Not when he'd finally gotten her attention.

"Uh, Ms. McSorley!"

She turned back to him. "Yeah?"

"As long as we're talking…do you think maybe my band could play you a quick song?"

The crowd burst into laughter. But it wasn't long before their giggles grew into a smattering of clapping hands, which soon turned into a rousing round of encouraging applause.

Ms. McSorley gave B.J. a glistening smile. "You want to play me a song?"

"Yes, ma'am," B.J. said.

"Right here?"

"Yes, ma'am. I mean, we've brought all our instruments and stuff."

"Let him play!" a voice shouted from the crowd.

"Right *on*! Let's hear the kid!" another voice agreed.

Scattered chants of "*LET HIM PLAY! LET HIM PLAY!*" began to fill the alley as Ms. McSorley scanned B.J. from head to toe. She silenced the entire crowd with one wave of her hand.

"You know what, B.J.?" she said. "I really dig your T-shirt, man. And I would be honored to hear your song."

"*WOOOOOOOOOOO!*" the crowd hollered.

B.J. had no idea what his T-shirt had to do with it, but he couldn't have cared less. He whirled around to his band and waved his hands wildly to beckon them over. Unfortunately, while he'd been pleading with Ms. McSorley, his band had apparently turned into petrified zombies. They were glued in place, eyes glazed over, arms dangling at their sides.

Jann had lost every ounce of cool in his body. The helpless look on his face made him look much younger or maybe it was just the first time he had actually looked his age.

"Guys." The veins were bulging from B.J.'s neck as he tried to shake them from their zombie trances. "Guys. Amps over here. *Dudes. Now!*"

He finally had to run over and physically wrangle them all toward the D.O.G, making sure they pulled along their amps and instruments. He tugged Lola out of Jann's scuffed black case, hung her over Jann's paralyzed shoulder, and handed KeVonne his bass. But there was still a problem. Layla had no drums. Undaunted, B.J. sprinted to the tin trash can behind them, flipped it over, and dumped the repellent mess of garbage on the ground. He raced back to Layla and placed the upside-down tin drum before her, unraveling the microphone he'd stuffed in his pocket and plugging into one of the little amps.

He blew into the mic. "Test, one-two, one-two." His voice carried to both ends of the alley. It brought the strangest combination of terror and exhilaration to his chest. "Okay," he panted into the mic. "'Atlantic City,' guys. A-one-two-three-four..."

Dead silence.

B.J. turned back to Jann, confused. The guitar was supposed to open the song, but Jann wasn't moving a muscle. He'd turned into a leather jacket–wearing deer in headlights.

"What's the problem?" B.J. whispered.

Jann pasted a nervous smile on his face and began nodding robotically to the crowd. Another wave of titters rippled through the audience.

B.J. backed up toward him. "*What* is the *problem*, Tweetles?"

"Forgot the song," Jann mumbled through his clenched smile.

"What? We rehearsed it for two hours."

"*Forgot song*," Jann repeated. "Need. Charts."

Jann had been reduced to speaking in Frankenstein. B.J. could hardly comprehend it, but Jann seemed even more nervous than he was. How was that possible?

"Where's the *music*?" B.J. whispered.

"Thought you would bring it."

"*No*," B.J. groaned. "No, no, no, no. What do we do *now*?"

"*You're* the master," Jann whispered.

"What?"

"You're the master of the art of rocking. Do a different song. What, do you only have one song?"

The answer, of course, was yes. *Yes, Jann, I only have one song, and it's not even my song.* But that wouldn't do. Not here. Not now.

"Come on," Jann whispered. "Just start something the D.O.G. will like. Something simple. I'll catch up."

The sweat was pouring off B.J.'s face like melted butter.

Something the D.O.G will like? I don't even know any other songs by heart.

But that wasn't true. There was one other song. One original song that he knew by heart because it had been hammered into his head over the last six weeks. And the more he thought about that song, the more this moment seemed like fate.

He turned back to the Daughters of Glenda and the restless crowd. "Ladies and gentlemen," he announced into the mic, "this is not a song about Taco Bell. This is a song about a war between dogs. In the future."

"*WOOOOOOOOOOOO!!!!*"

All they'd needed to hear was the word "dog," and they were whipped into an instant frenzy. "*Woof, woof, woof, woof...*"

A spark of recognition flashed across KeVonne's eyes. He knew the song B.J. meant because he'd heard it for the last six weeks too—every time he'd come to visit Jayson "Hot Wings" Levine. He and B.J. shared a split second of eye contact and then they let it rip out of sheer desperation...

Uh-huh, uh-huh, uh-huh
Just run for the BORDER
Uh-huh, uh-huh, uh-huh
You're a taco SNORTER
Bad chihuahua, don't snort the taco, don't snort the TACO...

It began as just a bass and vocal duet, but Layla caught on to the rhythm as quickly as she could. She pulled some timpani mallets from her messenger bag and started whaling on her trash can, smashing it like a piñata with candy trapped inside.

And finally, at long last, Jann broke out of his nervous deep freeze and followed Kev's chord changes, picking up the song in just a few bars. The amazing thing was, once Jann actually got a grip on the changes, his aggressive, rapid-fire guitar playing began to make "Dog Wars" sound almost cool. Even if it did have some of Dad's absolute worst lyrics in history…

"Something doesn't feel right
There's puppies in a gun fight
Warrior terrier, his jet pack on
He's gonna fly through the sky dropping terrier poop bombs
WHY oh WHY must a terrier groove on war?

Uh-huh, uh-huh
Just run for the border
Uh-huh, uh-huh, uh-huh
It's a new world order
Get me out of this DOG WAR, COME ON
We're all dogs, man, what are we fighting for?
We're all dogs, man, what are we fighting for?

B.J. was trying his best to imitate his father, but the deeper he fell into the song, the more he noticed sounds coming from his throat that he'd never heard before—sounds that must have been lying dormant in some locked box deep inside his chest for most of his childhood. Sounds that came dangerously close to *actual singing…*

A killer bichon frise with tear gas and pepper spray
Afghan hounds flyin' jets at the speed of sound
Labrador with a flak jacket strapped with C4
What are we fighting for?

He'd kept his eyes tightly shut for the entire song, but when he forced himself to peek, he could not believe what he saw. The alley had turned into a mini mosh pit. Gangs of wide-bottomed, middle-aged fans were bouncing off each other like chubby bumper cars, raising their devil horns high in the air. Even Christina McSorley and the D.O.G. had begun to bounce in place.

And when Jann finally stepped forward, the great Jann Solo was reborn. He and Lola came out of the bridge with the oddest, most unpredictable guitar solo, bringing the impromptu performance to a whole other level of awesome bizarreness.

It was so utterly surreal, B.J. didn't want it to end. He wanted the song to last for hours. Some part of him knew that this moment might never be repeated. He might be experiencing the last greatest moment of his life at the tender age of thirteen. But if there was one thing he'd learned from listening to his father, it was this: there were few things on Earth quite as unbearable as a song that went on for too long. He had to let it end.

Get me out of this DOG WAR, COME ON
We're all dogs, man, what are we fighting for?
We're all dogs, man, what are we fighting FOR?
OOOWWWWW!

He screamed out the highest final note he could, as Jann twanged one last hanging chord.

And then there was silence. Pure silence.

The crowd had no reaction. After all that moshing and barking and hooting, they'd gone as still as a picture. B.J. could feel his body shrinking. He could feel his heart slowly shriveling up and dying.

But the silence didn't last. It was as if someone had launched a silent firecracker in the air that finally landed in the alley with a *kaboom* of thunderous applause. The roar of the crowd ricocheted off the narrow brick walls with such brute force that B.J. had to cover both of his ears. KeVonne and Layla charged at him, collapsing on him and knocking him to his knees. He tried to catch his breath, but it was impossible.

In the chaos of the celebration, B.J. searched the crowd for Albino Paulie, but he had disappeared—probably too intimidated by Christina McSorley's queenly presence.

And that was exactly what it felt like. As Ms. McSorley stepped toward B.J. on his knees, it felt like she was his rock and roll queen,and he was her loyal subject, kneeling on the black pavement, hoping to be knighted in the alley behind the Castle Fillmore.

"B.J." She leaned down to him, her long, elegant arms outstretched. "How *old* are you guys?"

"Thirteen," B.J. said between short breaths.

"Fourteen," Jann chimed in, raising his hand.

"Well, you all just blew my forty-five-year-old mind." She lifted B.J. back to his feet and reached into the pocket of her feathered coat, pulling out a small stack of what looked like silver concert tickets with gold writing. But B.J. knew exactly what they were. He knew because it had been foretold in the book.

He had all but given up on that infernal book just three short minutes ago, but now...now everything had changed. Now he was convinced that the thing was straight-up gospel. Now he could feel it in his gut and his throat, and deep in his bones. His destiny was coming true.

"You guys *have* to come to the Hall of Fame party," Ms. McSorley said, handing him a short stack of tickets. "Just for a few minutes. I don't want you staying out too late. Are all your parents here?"

"Oh yes, ma'am," B.J. lied. "My folks are waiting for us just around the corner. They're huge fans by the way."

"Well, there are some private buses outside that can take you all to the event," she said. "Maybe you'll play us one more song when we get there, B.J.?"

"Oh *yes*, ma'am," he said, staring down at the ticket in awe.

ADMIT ONE.

BENEFIT FOR THE ROCK AND ROLL HALL OF FAME.

It might have said "Hall of Fame," but B.J. knew what it was really. It was his ticket to the Temple of Rock. Maybe even his ticket to the Holy Land.

★ ★ ★

"You kids looking for the bus to the Hall of Fame?"

A crinkly old woman had stepped in front of B.J. She was wearing a sleeveless Daughters of Glenda tour jacket and a faded red bandanna.

"Yes, ma'am," B.J. said. "We have passes for the party."

He handed the old woman his gold and silver passes, and she held them with her thin, bony fingers. "Okay. Cool beans," she said. "Follow me."

Cool beans?

She led them to a large silver tour bus that was parked across the street from the other buses on 17th. This must have been a special bus for the VIPs! B.J. couldn't help feeling like he'd officially reached rock star status—even if this Cinderella fantasy could only last for one night.

The old lady directed them up the narrow steps of the bus, and they made their way to the back, laying down their equipment and dropping into cushy chairs with sighs of relief. The old lady climbed the stairs and stood by the steering wheel. "Everyone get comfy!" she announced. "It's a bit of a ride uptown, but I'm going to get you there just as fast as I can. I'm Tiffani Bustamani by the way—that's Tiffani with an I—and I'll be your driver for the evening."

B.J. pulled his phone halfway out of his pocket. Mom's second text had come in.

MomCell: Are they putting you in the taxi now?

BJCell: Almost, yeah. But there's a lot of traffic, Mom. Might be a little bit later than I thought. They gave me some rainbow cookies to bring home!

MomCell: Will you just hurry back please? You know how I worry.

He shoved his phone back in his pocket. He really did hate to make his mother worry, but missing his shot at the Temple of Rock simply wasn't an option.

Tiffani settled into the driver's seat and adjusted herself

numerous times on the beaded seat cover. Then she pulled the bus door shut and cranked up the motor.

"Wait, aren't there more VIPs coming?" B.J. asked from the back.

"Oh, it's a shuttle service," Tiffani called back, using all the strength in her mushy arms to steer away from the curb and out onto Irving Place. "We'll be going back and forth from the party all night. You just kick back, son. I'll let you know when we're halfway there. *HAH!* Get it? I dig that T-shirt, man."

B.J. still had no idea why everyone loved his "We're Halfway There" T-shirt so much. He turned to Layla for her thoughts, but Layla's head had fallen against the window, her spiky bangs and her tiny pixie nose smushed up against it. Her body must have been so drained that it simply went into Emergency Snooze Mode. The faint, airy buzz of her mini-snores brought a little smile to the corner of his mouth. He hit the recline button on his armrest and leaned all the way back in his chair.

The bus grew very quiet as they began to cruise up Third Avenue. The whirring of the engine was the only sound. It was B.J.'s first truly peaceful moment since walking into Layla's apartment more than three hours earlier.

He closed his eyes and took advantage of this golden opportunity to relive his wondrous, life-changing night in the alley behind the Fillmore New York.

CHAPTER seven

A nasty bump in the road opened his eyes.

He tried to shake off the fog of sleep, but he was stuck in that half-napping, backseat daze. He knew he'd probably fall back asleep any second.

The first thing he noticed was Layla's hair. It was only an inch from his face, smelling of jasmine and mint and ginger. Her hands were clasped around his elbow, and she was resting her head on his shoulder. Having her this close made his stomach feel too light—like there were small furry creatures scampering around under his rib cage.

He carefully turned his head across the aisle and saw that KeVonne and Jann had fallen asleep in their seats too. He turned back toward the window, trying not to let his chin brush too heavily across Layla's hair.

The dark road was rolling by, lit up by the bus's dim amber

headlights. There was just enough moonlight outside to see the blur of the metal highway railing, and the masses of tall trees, and the wide-open fields beyond the road, and…

Wait.

Wide-open fields? Since when does Manhattan have wide-open fields?

He shook off a layer of sleepiness and leaned closer to the window, pushing Layla with him until he could see the bright-green reflecting road sign speeding toward him.

I-80 CLEVELAND 345 MILES

Cleveland?

Layla woke with a frightened gasp, nearly knocking the back of her head against the window. "Whah?" she cried. "Wha's going on?"

B.J. didn't realize he'd actually yelled the word "Cleveland." He thought he'd only screamed it in his mind. He jumped from his seat, nearly smashing his head on one of the overhead reading lights. "That sign said Cleveland."

"What are you talking about?" Jann asked, lazily. His leather jacket rustled as he stretched his long arms, waking from a deep sleep.

"Look outside!" B.J. shouted, jogging up and down the bus's narrow aisle. He crouched for a better view through the polarized windows. "We're not in the city anymore."

"Yeah, right," Jann snorted. "Dude, I only fell asleep for, like…" Jann's jaw dropped as he looked out at the moonlit highway.

Layla slid over in her seat and shook KeVonne's shoulder. "Ke*Vonne.* Wake up."

"Whopper junior," Kev mumbled sleepily. "Bacon cheese."

"Kev, get *up*, dude." B.J. smacked him in the shoulder.

"Whassup? What's wrong?"

B.J. finally remembered that someone was actually driving the bus. He raced to the front and leaned down next to Tiffani Bustamani in her red bandanna. She was gazing out at the black horizon, crushing the pedal to the metal, humming herself a little tune.

"What are you *doing?*" he asked frantically.

"Huh?" Tiffani smiled and leaned back, pointing at her right ear. "Sorry, son. Lost the hearing in this ear at a Skid Row show in '89."

"Where are we *going?*" B.J. placed his mouth directly next to her ear.

"Oh! Hall of Fame, of course!"

"But we're not even in New York!"

"You said it!" she nodded. "The Hall of Fame's gonna *rock*! Cleveland, U.S. of A., baby! *Woof, woof, woof, woof!*"

"No, not *rock. YORK.* We're supposed to be at the Hall of Fame, *New York*. Not *Cleveland! NEW YORK CIT-EE.*"

Tiffani furrowed her brow. She'd finally understood him over the loud din of the bus's rumbling engine. She sniffed a few times through her double-pierced nose and then looked to her left and then her right, taking in the view of the barren highway. "Okay, see, now, that's my bad."

"Your *bad*?"

Layla ran up from behind. "What's going on?"

B.J. was so panicked he could hardly move the muscles in his face. "She's…She's driving us to the Hall of Fame in Cleveland. She says it's her bad."

"Her *bad*?" Layla squeaked.

"Totally my bad," Tiffani said, raising her hand. "Oh boy. I do sincerely apologize, kids. I ain't been altogether right in the brain since the Whitesnake show at Red Rocks '86. Oh man, the '60s were a crazy time."

"Oh my god," B.J. breathed. "Oh my God, oh my God, oh my God…" He darted his eyes down to the clock on the bus's dashboard.

10:50 p.m.

"Oh my God, oh my God, oh my God…"

He dropped down in the front seat of the bus, both hands cupping his head. "I'm dreaming this, right? I'm totally dreaming this. This is the nightmare where I go back to Cleveland. That's all this is. It has to be."

Layla plopped down next to him as Jann and Kev came rushing up to the front.

"Dude, we just passed a sign for Stroudsburg, Pennsylvania," Jann said. "Can anyone tell me *why* we just passed a sign for *Stroudsburg, Pennsylvania*?"

"I'm gonna gas her up in Stroudsburg," Tiffani explained. "The station's just up ahead. Then we can clear up our little tour glitch, m'kay?"

"*Little tour glitch?*" B.J. was still gripping his head. "We're *a hundred* miles from New York! It's eleven o'clock at night! My mom probably thinks I'm dead!"

"Well, give her a call, Mitch," Tiffani said. "Tell her you ain't dead and we just took ourselves a little accidental detour."

"An accidental…? Who's *Mitch*? Is there something wrong with your brain, lady?"

But she'd already answered that question. There was something seriously wrong with her brain. It had been blown to bits by the likes of Skid Row and Whitesnake, whoever they were.

B.J. looked down at his jeans pocket. He knew he needed to call his mother immediately to tell her that he wasn't dead, but once she found out where he was, she was going to kill him anyway. He just needed a minute to figure things out—just a little more time before he tried to explain the unexplainable.

Tiffani heaved the steering wheel and sent them veering off

onto a winding rotary exit. They bounced over two big speed bumps and then cruised toward a vast parking lot.

A few parked buses were scattered in front of a dilapidated bus station, which looked more like a gas station. A run-down neon sign was nailed to the roof.

STROUDSBURG TATION

The S in "station" had probably blown out ten years ago and no one had bothered to climb the roof to fix it.

The three buses in the lot looked like they'd been out of commission for years. They sat there like huge dead carcasses under a row of flickering fluorescent lights.

Tiffani pulled into one of the open spots and shut off the motor, standing up out of her seat and stretching her arms and legs like an old dog on a patch of backyard grass.

"Why don't you all step on out and stretch?" she said. "I'm going see if that rascally old coffee machine still works." She cranked open the door and skipped down the bus's steps.

"Tiffani, wait a minute! Jeez!" B.J. followed her out into the unexpectedly cold autumn air, wrapping his arms tightly around his chest. "You can't just *leave* us out here in the middle of nowhere! We have to get back to New York. We have to get back to our parents."

Tiffani placed her hand gently on B.J.'s lanky shoulder. "Let's dial down the panic there, Mitch. I'm just grabbing a coffee and taking a little trip to the ladies' for a Number Two. I shouldn't be too long depending on how that goes, m'kay?"

"But..."

"Aw, *nuts*, nature calls, Mitch! Too many Fig Newtons—you know how it is!" Tiffani made a beeline for the bus station door, whipped it open, and let it slam behind her.

Layla, Jann, and Kev stumbled out onto the gray asphalt, darting their heads in all directions like lost lambs. Their breaths formed visible white plumes in the crisp, cool air.

"What did she say?" Layla asked.

B.J. could only stand there, stupefied. "She said she had to go Number Two."

"Dude, what the *heck* is going on?" KeVonne started zipping up all the zippers on his paratrooper jumpsuit to try and stay warm.

"What's going on?" Jann's face was turning bright red with anger. "We just got kidnapped by Tiffani Bustamani, *that's* what's going on! I'm calling my dad." Jann reached into his coat pocket and felt around for his cell phone. "Where's my cell?" He checked every other pocket in his jacket and then went through the front and back pockets of his jeans twice. "Dude, *where* is my cell?"

B.J. reached into his pocket and searched for his cell phone too, but all he could feel was a pack of Trident gum. "I don't have mine either."

They all started rummaging desperately through their pockets as Jann turned to the bus station door, his eyes slowly closing into tiny slits. "*Tiffani!*"

He took off toward the bus station doors, and B.J. instinctively chased after him, turning back to Layla and Kev. "You guys get back on the bus!"

When he turned around, Jann had already increased his lead by ten paces. "Jann, wait up! Don't do anything crazy!"

"Crazy?" Jann yelled back, tugging the station door open. "Tiffani Bustamani just drove me to Stroudsburg, Pennsylvania, and stole my cell phone! Don't talk to *me* about crazy!"

The door shut behind him.

★ ★ ★

Jann had disappeared by the time B.J. swung open the cracked glass doors of the Stroudsburg Station.

"Jann…? Jann, where are you?"

"Just find us a pay phone," Jann's voice echoed from somewhere across the drafty room. "I'll find Bustamani!"

B.J. took his first look at the crusty interior of the station, and he fell back against the frosty doors. The station was larger than it looked from the outside. Maybe because there wasn't a single soul in sight. It was one big, smelly, fluorescent ghost town.

The yellowing linoleum floor reeked of chlorine and mildew. The white walls had faded to a dank shade of dirt-gray. There were a few rows of rusty orange metal seats, folded shut, and a row of dented brown vending machines, including Tiffani's "rascally old coffee machine." But there was no Tiffani. And now there was no Jann.

Pay phone. Just find a pay phone and call Mom.

It was amazing how quickly you could go from avoiding your mother like the plague to desperately pining for your mommy.

He could see a sliver of the dimly lit hallway around the corner from the vending machines. He wondered if there might be some old pay phones in that hallway, but he also wondered if there might be an axe murderer with a prosthetic leg or perhaps the Stroudsburg Strangler (he was absolutely sure there was a Stroudsburg Strangler).

"Jann?" he called out again. "Jann, where are you?"

Nothing but windy silence. He'd have to check out the hallway himself, even if every bone in his body was telling him to run back to the bus and wait for Tiffani to finish pooping.

Step by hesitant step, he dragged himself across the puke-stained floor. (He couldn't prove the stains were puke; he just had a feeling that a lot of puking had taken place at the Stroudsburg Station.) When he reached the corner, he took a deep breath and leaned his head around for a better look.

No pay phones in the dingy hallway—just restrooms. Jann must have run right by them when he stormed in.

He crept slowly toward the dark-red ladies' room door and leaned his ear against it.

"Tiffani?" he whispered. "Tiffani, are you in there?"

No reply. He knocked lightly on the door and then cracked it open an inch. "Ms. Bustamani? Everything going all right in there? We'd really like to start heading back to New York now."

No reply again. This seemed like a desperate enough situation to warrant throwing good manners to the wind, so B.J. swung the door open and stepped onto the chipped white tiles of the ladies' room. "Tiffani...?"

He crouched down and peered under the three rusty bathroom stalls. Not a lady-foot in sight. The room was empty.

A sick chill went through his stomach. *This is bad. Something is very wrong here.*

He backed up to leave, but as he neared the door, he heard heavy-booted footsteps clomping down the hall.

The echoing footsteps grew louder and louder until they ceased right in front of the ladies' room door. B.J.'s legs began to tremble, and he couldn't make them stop. He could see the shadow of two feet standing motionless beneath the doorway. He could hear heavy breathing on the other side, but the figure wasn't moving.

"Tiffani?" he croaked.

A hand smashed the door, which swung open in a gust of pure chaos. B.J. tried to leap out of the way, but the hand grabbed hold of his shoulder. He wanted to scream, but another pale, calloused hand smothered his mouth.

"Do *not* scream," a deep, scratchy voice whispered from behind.

B.J. flailed his arms and legs to escape, but at the same time, he was thinking *I know that voice.*

It couldn't be. There was just no way. But as the calloused hands spun him around and shook him still, he could not deny the face of his captor.

Albino Paulie. This human wad of tissue paper was *everywhere.* Had he seriously followed their bus all the way to *Pennsylvania*?

Paulie kept his hand firmly strapped over B.J.'s mouth. "Listen to me, Scarecrow. I don't care if it's a perfect G-sharp or an A above middle C, I don't want to hear that scream again. Do you understand me? Nod if you understand me."

B.J. nodded as his body went limp with fear.

"Good," Paulie whispered. "Now, I'm gonna let go of your mouth, but if you scream, then we're all going down, kid. Nod if you understand me."

B.J. didn't have the foggiest idea what he meant, but he nodded just so Paulie would take his hand off his mouth.

"Now you need to listen to me real good," Paulie said. "I been trying to protect yous from afar, but that ain't workin' out, so now we gotta do this up close and personal."

"Protect me from—?"

Paulie crushed his hand over B.J.'s mouth again. "We do this *quiet-like.* They've got this whole place surrounded."

"Huh?" B.J. could only use muted animal noises to express his confusion. Through Paulie's smothering fingers, he managed to ask "*Who's* got the place surrounded?"

"Who do you think?" Paulie said. "B.L.A.S.T. They're circling this place like vultures right now. God, you still don't get it, do you?"

B.J. shook his head a most definite "no." He absolutely, one hundred percent, did *not* get it.

"You're doing every single thing they want you to do, Scarecrow," Paulie whispered. "I don't know how they're getting you to do it, but you're falling right into their trap, and if you don't come with me right now, then you're a *dead* scarecrow. We gotta *move*, brother. My bike's outside. Let's go."

Before B.J. could argue, Paulie was dragging him out of the bathroom, back through the crusty main room of the bus station, toward an out-of-the-way maintenance exit. He kicked open the gray metal doors with his boot and pulled B.J. past an unholy-smelling yellow dumpster, toward his parked Harley-Davidson.

"Okay, wait a second!" B.J. threw on the brakes and tried to rip himself away from Paulie's grip, forcing them into a tug-of-war with his arm. "Just *hold* on, okay? I have no clue what is going on here. I feel like I'm having a bad dream, except I don't think so because of that disgusting smell."

"Oh, it ain't a dream, kid, but you're gonna wish it was if you don't get on this bike right now."

"There is *no* way I am getting on that bike. I need to get back to my band. I need to call my mom, and I need to find our bus driver so she can drive us back to the city."

"You're not thinking this *through*, kid." Paulie glanced nervously in all directions. "Your bus driver's *gone*. All she had to do was get you out here. Her job is done. And they don't care about your band. All they care about is *you*. I'm sure you felt like the king of da world after your little breakout performance back at the Fillmore, but you just sealed your own doom, fool. I tried to stop it, but you just had to rock out, didn't you? You just had to find your inner Bayonne. Well, now they know it's you."

"My inner what? What are you *talking* about?"

"I'll explain later. Just get on!"

"No, let me *go*." B.J. broke free and made for the station, but Paulie snatched him back up.

"Hey! What did I just tell you? B.L.A.S.T. has you surrounded. Thirty seconds and this place is going to be a war zone."

"What do you mean 'a war zone'?"

The sudden assault on B.J.'s eardrums was like two nuclear warheads exploding simultaneously. He dropped to his knees and covered his ears as the world became a swirl of toxic black smoke.

It sounded like a fleet of howling jet planes dive-bombing

from the sky and crisscrossing the back lot. But as he squinted into their blinding white headlights, he could see that they were motorcycles. Chrome and black rubber invaded from all sides. Leather and white beards flashed all around him, but the only thing he could really make out was the bandannas—a storm of red bandannas, rippling in the wind as the hulking Harleys circled and revved and roared.

Paulie dropped to the ground for cover, but B.J. wasn't about to wait and see what happened next. He shielded his mouth and took off through the noxious smoke—back through the entire puke-stained station and out to the front parking lot.

KeVonne and Layla were waiting anxiously by the entrance. They must have run from the bus when they heard all the commotion out back.

Layla grabbed B.J.'s arm. "What's going on back there?"

B.J. whipped his head to the left and right. He had to make a split-second decision. If they got back on Tiffani's bus, they'd be trapped without a driver. If they ran back into the station, they'd be that much closer to the Hard Rock Terminators.

But the choice was made for him. The storm of red bandannas swerved around the corner and came to a screeching halt. The bikers labored to climb off their bulky bikes, and they began galloping toward B.J., their paunchy stomachs bouncing with every stride.

"Come on!" B.J. grabbed Layla's hand, and they took off with KeVonne.

They were running blind. No idea where they were headed or where they could even turn—just flat-out running from the psycho bikers, who were surprisingly fast for old dudes in ludicrously tight leather pants. Kev was nearly toppling over on his Bootsy Boots with every other step. B.J. and Layla each grabbed hold of one of his arms and basically carried him as they ran. Layla was surprisingly strong for such a tiny thing. All that drum pounding must have really strengthened her forearms.

"Over here!" B.J. shouted, leading them behind one of the parked abandoned buses. But as they turned the corner, they quickly discovered that this particular bus was far from abandoned.

"What the bloody hell is going on here?!"

A dwarf with a cockney accent was leaning against the side of the bus, holding a long, old-fashioned cigarette holder with half a cigarette still burning at its tip. He had a stubbly brown beard and wavy brown hair down to his shoulders. He was dressed in a flowing white muslin shirt, a lavender silk scarf, and purple spandex pants embroidered with gold moons and stars.

B.J. was at a loss for words, as were his bandmates. A little person in purple spandex was the last thing they'd expected to see. But this was no time to be choosy about their savior.

"We need your help," B.J. said. "They're after us."

"Who's after you, mate?" Purple Pants asked.

"*Them.*" B.J. pointed behind him.

Purple Pants leaned his head around the bus and saw the biker stampede approaching.

"Good God." His eyes bulged as he ducked back behind the bus and stomped out his cigarette. "All right, get on," he said. He quickly began helping the kids onto his bus.

"We have to get back to New York," B.J. said as he was rushed up the steps.

"Yeah, cheers, mate. We're headed east. Just get on the *bus*, man. They're bloody *fast* for a bunch of old coots."

"No, wait!" B.J. froze at the top step. "Jann. Where's Jann?"

"I thought he was behind us," Kev said.

"*No*. He's still in the station looking for Tiffani! I gotta go get him."

"No, Levine. *Wait.*" Layla tried to hold him back, but he was already leaping down the bus's steps.

KeVonne jumped down after him. "All right, go around the side, Beej! I'll create a diversion."

Kev bravely jumped back out in front of the biker stampede. "Over here, you freaky H.O.G.s!" He wiggled his pear-shaped jumpsuit to get their attention, and then he dove back behind the dwarf's bus and climbed up the steps.

B.J. crouched down as low as his tall frame would allow. He

slid along the side of Purple Pants's bus, crept along the rear fenders of two more empty buses, and then dove for the station's east wall, pressing his shoulders up against the cold cement as he tried to catch his breath. He could hear the bikers gathering around Purple Pants's bus like a lynch mob, banging angrily on the door.

"Open this door, man! Open up! We just wanna tawk to the skinny kid!"

B.J. raced along the station's east wall, all the way to the back lot. Albino Paulie's Harley had disappeared. B.J. bulleted back into the station through the maintenance doorway and began his mad search for Jann.

"Jann, where are you, dude? Jann?" He ducked into every grimy nook and corner he could find. He rechecked the ladies' room and barreled into the disgusting men's room, pinching his nostrils shut. "Jann, forget about your cell phone, dude! Forget about Tiffani. We have a ride!"

Still not a peep in response—just the nagging sound of the wind, snaking its way through the empty station. Where on Earth was Jann? What had happened to him?

Oh God, what if B.L.A.S.T. got him? Or Tiffani?

Was Tiffani Bustamani really evil? Was her brain-dead groupie thing all an act? Was Albino Paulie really just trying to protect B.J.?

His mind spinning with those questions and about a hundred more, B.J. backed out the front doors empty handed. He'd searched every hall and corner and now his heart was filling with genuine dread for Jann. So much dread that he'd failed to notice the two men lying in wait for him on either side of the doorway.

"AAAAAAAAHHHHHHH!"

The two bikers were momentarily stunned by B.J.'s scream, but they regained their composure and grabbed hold of his arms, dragging him forward despite his attempts to dig his heels into the ground.

"What are you doing?" B.J. hollered. "What are you *doing*?"

It was hard to see anything in all the chaos. The man gripping his left arm had fluffy gray muttonchops sprouting from his cheeks and a studded bracelet on each wrist. B.J. caught a glimpse of the grungy T-shirt under his leather jacket. It had a picture of a piano keyboard with two chicken claws sticking out of the bottom. "Chicken Fingers," it said.

It was hard to see Chicken Fingers's face under his fluffy, gray muttonchops, but there was no mistaking the man gripping B.J.'s other arm.

Those bulging, bloodshot eyes. That long red, hobo goat beard. That leathery skin…

Merv.

"You left me no choice, Circus Boy," Merv said, his ancient vocal cords cracking with every word. "Now you're coming with us."

Merv and Chicken Fingers dragged B.J. violently across the

rugged asphalt. He was bucking and kicking to break free as they pulled him farther and farther from his friends.

"Okay, just chill, Merv!" B.J. pleaded. "I'll give you the book back, dude! No problem! It's back there in my backpack! I was just holding onto it for you!"

But Merv and Chicken Fingers weren't listening. They pulled B.J. toward their parked battalion of shiny bikes. He was sure they were going to throw him onto the back of one of the Harleys, but an old white Volkswagen van rocketed into view from around the corner and careened toward him in reverse. It spun out on its old gray tires and stopped short with a screech.

"We've got him!" Merv called to the van. "Open the doors, man! Grab his legs!"

The back doors of the van swung open as two more bikers jumped out and reached for B.J.'s legs, lifting him off the ground like a casualty of war. B.J. felt a surge of terror as they pulled his writhing body toward the van's shadowy interior.

"No, no, no. What are you doing? Let me go!"

They'd wrestled him halfway into the van when he got his first glimpse of the big black blur darting from Tiffani's bus. He craned his neck over Merv's pointy bandanna to get a better look at the dark figure charging up from behind, but he only saw a glimmer of fluorescent light reflecting off a shiny black weapon before the first blow came crashing down on Merv's head.

"*Oompf!*" Merv collapsed to the ground. He'd been hit with what looked like a giant black baseball bat. B.J. saw a flash of white writing on the bat as it rose up for its second blow, but when he actually read the word, he realized it wasn't a bat at all.

No! B.J. thought to himself in that split-second. *No, Jann, not Lola!*

But before he could protest, Jann raised Lola high over his shoulders, wielding her by the neck like the ultimate rocker, poised to close out his show with supreme destruction. He brought Lola down on Chicken Fingers's back, snapping her wooden neck clean off as Chicken Fingers bounced off the van's open door and sunk to the ground.

"Come on!" Jann yelled, grabbing B.J. and hurling the splintered remains of Lola's neck at the other two bikers.

"This way!" B.J. shouted, leading Jann in a full-throttle dash for Purple Pants's bus.

The bus had begun circling the parking lot in an attempt to shake off the mob of angry bikers. It picked up speed, breaking away from the gang and catching up alongside B.J. and Jann as they maintained a steady jog. It came to a hard stop and the door flew open.

"I've got you!" Layla hollered, locking onto B.J.'s arm and pulling him up the bus's steps. Once B.J. had his feet firmly planted, he reached for Jann and pulled him on too.

"We're in!" he shouted.

The bus driver pulled the door shut and floored the gas pedal, forcing the bus's motor to growl like an angry grizzly before it erupted into a high-pitched whir and shot away from the Stroudsburg Station.

The biker mob grew smaller and smaller in the rearview mirror as the bus swerved its way onto Interstate 80.

CHAPTER eight

They were all huddled together by the front of the bus: B.J., Layla, Kev, Jann, and Purple Pants. No one spoke at first. They just eyed each other with confusion, trying to catch their breath, trying to make sense of the last ten harrowing minutes, trying to figure out what might happen in the next ten.

The bus driver was maintaining a speed of 70 miles per hour as they cruised down the highway. He had long brown curly hair cascading down his back, and he wore a frilly white pirate shirt with the laces untied at the center, revealing his muscular chest.

Escape had been the only thing on B.J.'s mind until now. There'd been no time to ask himself whether it was really wise to hop on Purple Pants's bus without even knowing his name—without even knowing *why* he wore the purple pants or employed pirates.

Purple Pants was standing at the front of the bus's aisle, steadying himself between two armrests, his head no higher than the tops of the vinyl seats.

"The name's Terry," he said in his heavy British accent. "Terry the Wünder-Dwarf. And it ain't 'Wonder-Dwarf' like the white bread, aw'ight? I prefer the German pronunciation, '*Voon*-der Dwarf.' Now, which one of you blokes is gonna tell me what just happened back there?"

"I got *no* idea," KeVonne blurted out, reaching down to pull a Bootsy Boot off his aching foot. "Beej? You wanna tell us what just happened?"

B.J. remained silent. He kept his head hanging low, praying the river of adrenaline pumping through his veins wouldn't cause him to projectile vomit onto Terry the Wünder-Dwarf's head.

"Hey, it's cool, man," Terry said calmly. He could tell B.J. was too traumatized to speak. He patted B.J.'s stomach, which was not the greatest idea right now. "I been in my share of Barney when I was a young dodger too, mate."

Barney? It was hard enough to understand Terry's accent, let alone the weird words he was using.

Terry looked up at B.J.'s pale, clammy cheeks. "Relax, mate, aw'ight? You're safe wif us now. You're on the Wünder-Bus, man. You wanna tell me what just happened? Did you fall in love wif a biker's daughter? Is that why they was coming after ya?" He smiled and jabbed B.J.'s thigh with his elbow. "I been there, man. What's her name?"

"No, it's nothing like that," Layla said. "I mean, I don't think that's what it was."

"Then what *was* it?" Jann ripped off his leather jacket and hurled it to the floor. His white T-shirt was soaked under the arms with sweat. "*What* is your beef with hobo bikers, Levine? First that freaky albino at the Fillmore and now this? We could have died out there, dude! They could have run us over. They could have stuffed us all in that van and held us for hobo ransom or something!"

"I know that, Jann! You think I don't know that? This is all my fault, okay?" B.J. shoved his way past Terry and ran down the length of the bus, searching for a place to be alone.

The bus might have looked like a regular king-size greyhound from the outside, but inside, it looked more like some sort of hippie magician's studio apartment. The windows were all draped over with long purple scarves embroidered with gold moons and stars. Four shallow sleeper bunks were built into the rear of the bus, which seemed like B.J.'s only shot at privacy. He ripped back one of the bunk's glittery purple curtains—only to discover another muscle-dude in an unlaced pirate shirt and flannel pajama pants.

"Hey, I need my *sleep*, Terry," the pirate groaned. He slid the black sleep mask off his eyes and stared at B.J., bewildered, pulling the yellow foam earplugs from his ears. "You ain't Terry," he said with an accent just like Terry's.

"No," was all B.J. could think to say.

"Well, where the hell is Terry?" He rolled out of his bunk and climbed to his feet, rubbing his sleepy eyes and tossing his long red hair behind his shoulders with a flick of his head. He stared angrily down the aisle to the front of the bus. "Terry, is this another one of your *kids*, man? How many kids you *got*? We said no kids on the tour!"

"He ain't my kid, Graham," Terry called back. "We just had ourselves a situation, that's all. He needed our help, mate."

"Help wif what? Where did all these *kids* come from?"

Pirate Graham stormed up the aisle, leaving B.J. staring at his empty bunk. He felt so nauseous and exhausted that he simply climbed into the cramped little sleeper and pulled down the purple curtain. All he wanted to do was curl up in a ball and pretend that none of this was happening.

It wasn't long before Layla lifted the corner of the purple curtain and peeked into the narrow bunk. "Levine? Are you okay?"

"Oh yeah, I'm fine," he mumbled. He turned away and pressed his head against the wall. He could feel the entire bus vibrating as it absorbed the bumps in the highway.

"You don't sound fine," Layla said.

"Yeah, that's because I'm lying. That's pretty much all I do now."

"What's that supposed to mean?"

"Forget it," he said. "Layla, just don't hate me, all right?"

"Why would I hate you?"

"Because this is all my fault. All of it. Jann's right. I could have gotten you guys killed or kidnapped or I don't even know what. But don't worry, it's over now. I'm done with my stupid little quest. I'll just be an accountant like my mom wants."

Layla socked him in the leg. "Don't talk like that, Levine. What do you mean it's over?"

"Trust me, Layla, you wouldn't understand."

"Well, maybe I would." She peeked back at the crowd by the front of the bus and lowered her voice to a whisper. "Levine, do you think those bikers were from B.L.A.S.T.?"

"What?" Hearing Layla say that name was like a Taser in the back. He flipped over and locked his eyes with hers. "How do you know that name?"

"Re*lax*. I saw it in your book."

"How did you see my book?"

"Scooch over," she said.

"There's no room to scooch—"

"Just scooch over."

Layla lifted the curtain and climbed into the cramped little sleeper next to B.J. Now her toes were pressed against his knees, and their noses were just an inch short of touching, as they faced each other eye-to-eye in near darkness. B.J. felt those furry little creatures start to scamper around his chest again. This girl just didn't seem to care about the normal rules of boy-girl distance.

She pulled the book from the back pocket of her jeans and dropped it in the tiny sliver of space between them. "Look, I wasn't trying to go through your stuff or anything. It just happened while you were in the station. I wanted to give you that playlist I made you, so I unzipped your bag to put in the thumb drive and this book just dropped out. I know I shouldn't have looked at it, but I did because it looked weird, or cool, or, I don't know, both. Were those guys from B.L.A.S.T. or not?"

He felt so deeply embarrassed knowing she'd seen his "guide to rock supremacy," but at the same time, some part of him felt relieved. Keeping the book a secret had become a much lonelier prospect than he'd imagined. It was good to finally have someone to talk to.

He lowered his voice to a whisper too. "I'm pretty sure they were from B.L.A.S.T. At least, that's what Paulie said."

"Paulie? You mean freaky albino guy Paulie? You saw him *again*?"

"Yeah. He was inside the station."

"Shut *up*."

"I swear to God. He was inside the station. He wanted me to get on his bike with him. I think he was trying to save me."

"Wait, wait, wait…" Layla shook her head. "You're telling me the albino guy followed our bus all the way from New York?"

"I guess so.."

"Levine, what is going on here?"

"I don't *know*, Layla. I thought they just wanted their book back."

"I don't think they want the book, Levine. I think they want you."

Another sickening surge of adrenaline washed over him. Because she had to be right, didn't she? He remembered what Paulie said to him right before the B.L.A.S.T. invasion: "They don't care about your band. All they care about is you."

"But why?" B.J. was asking himself as much as he was asking Layla. "No, I don't even want to think about it anymore. All I want to do is go home. That's all I want to do."

"Go home? Are you nuts? You want to go home *now*?"

"Don't you?"

Layla grabbed the book and opened it to the first page. "Levine, I just read everything it said in this book, and I don't know if you've noticed, but everything it says in this book is *happening*. I mean, look…" She started flipping through each page. "You put our band together in less than a week." *Flip.*

"You led us to the D.O.G. You got the Daughters of Glenda to hear *us* play, and we showed them our enormous talents." *Flip.* "And then we headed for the Temple of Rock. That's like code for the Hall of Fame, right?"

"How did you get that so fast?"

"What? It's obvious."

"Yeah," he lied, "it didn't take me that long to figure out either."

"The point is, we were headed for the Temple of Rock, and I think we might still be headed to this Holy Land place! Don't you want to know what that *is*?"

B.J. couldn't believe how into this whole thing Layla was. He thought she'd be devastated by the attack. He thought she'd be a whimpering mess—begging for home like he was, but the more he thought about it, the more he realized that "whimpering mess" wasn't very Layla-like. He obviously had a lot more to learn about Layla Ginsberg.

"And look," she went on. She flipped to Chapter 4's title page. "Look what it says here. 'He embarked on a long and arduous journey to the Holy Land—traveling *far from home* and enduring many trials.' Hel-*lo?* What do you call this? I don't know what the Fire Pit is, but I bet you we'll find out. I think this is, like, destiny. Don't you believe in destiny?"

He'd believed in it for a second, when Christina McSorley

handed him that stack of gold and silver tickets, but now he wasn't so sure.

"I don't know," he said.

"Well, I believe in destiny, and I don't care how corny it sounds. I think us meeting was destiny, Levine. Like the way we were both in the basement that first day of school. Like the way you heard me playing the drums before we'd even met or the way I wanted to join the band when we'd only talked for five minutes."

"No, wait a minute." He pointed at her. "You didn't want to join the band. You ran away like I had some kind of disease."

"Ugh, Levine. You're such an idiot sometimes." She swatted his finger away. "I ran away because I was afraid."

"Afraid of what?"

Layla rolled her eyes and turned away. "Look, I know I said I was playing with a few different bands and everything, but the truth is...I've been kicked out of every band I've ever auditioned for. Usually after one rehearsal."

"What?"

"Sometimes they even stop me right at the beginning of a rehearsal and ask me to leave because their folks are complaining about the noise. They call me 'Layla the Whala,' Levine. Because of the way I whale on the drums. I play so loud that no one can stand it."

"You've *never* been in a band before?"

"Not for more than a day. I only took one drum lesson in my life, and the only thing the guy taught me was to play eight on the hat, one and three on the kick, two and four on the snare, and to hit *really hard*. That's the only way I know how to play. No one will play with me. Even in the practice room, people always come in and tell me to shut up. I thought that's what you were going to do, but you didn't. You *liked* the fact that my drums sounded like demon footsteps. You *wanted* to play with me. That's never happened before. That has to be fate, right? The way we met? I think that'll be the story we tell people when they ask how we got together."

"How we...?"

"The *band*." She socked him in the shoulder again. "That's how the *band* got together. God, what's it going to take to convince you? What, do you need another sign or something?"

Terry suddenly peeked his big noggin through the curtain, startling them both. "What are you two lovebirds doin' in here?" He flashed B.J. a sly grin and winked at him. "Nice one, mate. I'll just leave you two alone then—"

"No, it's not like that!" B.J. knocked his head on the upper bunk as he tried to get up. "I'm mean, we're not...We're just..."

"Yeah, I think I get the picture, li'l big man. Anyhoo, I just had a nice little chat wif your mates up front, and they filled me in on the whole situation, so here's the deal. I'm gonna give you kids my cellie so you can all call your mums and tell 'em you're safe and sound and comfy-cozy. You tell 'em that old Terry's gonna take proper care of ya and that the Wünder-Bus will get you back to the Big Apple in a jiff. We just gotta make one little stop on the way is all."

"Stop?" B.J. didn't like the sound of that. "Stop where?"

"Well, we was on our way to a gig," Terry said, "and I'm afraid we can't miss it."

"A gig? You mean like a magic show?"

"A magic show?" Terry turned to Layla. "What's he on about?"

"You're not a magician?" B.J. asked. "You know…the Merlin pants?"

"*Merlin* pants?" Terry tugged at his purple spandex leggings. "These ain't *Merlin* pants, kid, these is *rock and roll* pants! You blokes just happen to be on tour with Terry the Wünder-Dwarf and the Pirates of Munchausen!"

"Don't mind Levine," Layla said. "He's still just a little freaked out, that's all."

"Yeah, aw'ight," Terry said, cooling down. "No worries, darlin'. So, your mates tell me you're all budding rock and rollers too, ay? What's the name of your outfit?"

B.J. shook his head. "No, we're not really a band. We're just—"

"The Good Supreme," Layla interrupted. "We're called the Good Supreme."

Terry grinned. "*Nice*. I dig it."

"Thanks," Layla said. "We think it's pretty cool too. So, where's this gig at?"

"Oh, you're gonna have a *blast*," Terry said. "It's this rockin' little underground club in Philly called the Fire Pit."

Layla gasped. She turned to B.J., eyes ablaze, and elbowed him hard in the stomach. "Is *that* enough of a sign for you?"

Sammy, I know I said I would tell you every detail of my story from now on, but I think I should skip the part where I called my mom at eleven o'clock at night to tell her I wasn't dead. Let's just say that she was very happy I was alive but <u>very</u> unhappy that I was in Pennsylvania on a tour bus with Terry the Wunder-Dwarf.

The good news is, Mom and Mrs. Hammond called off the NYPD! And after a very, very long talk with Terry, Mom agreed to let him drive us back to the Port Authority bus station in New York, where all our parents would meet us. He even convinced her to let him make his one little stop in Philly before he brought us home.

We all thought it was best not to tell our folks that Terry's one little stop was at a rock club called the Fire Pit. You've seen the Fire Pit, Sammy, so I think you can understand why we skipped that part.

CHAPTER nine

The Fire Pit. It sounded like it was either an old-fashioned barbecue joint or some kind of flaming hellscape buried deep underground. It turned out to be both.

Yes, B.J. was sitting at a bar. They all were. An actual bar. Three thirteen-year-olds, one fourteen-year-old, a little person in spandex pants, and two pirates. They were lined up in a row, sitting on ratty old barstools, staring at themselves in the long, washed-out mirror behind a wall of amber whisky bottles. The smell of sawdust wafted up from the floor mixed with the horrible stench of stale beer. The howl of distorted guitars echoed from a stage in the corner of the cavernous black room, rattling B.J.'s eardrums.

The band onstage was called Tony's Hyundai, and every one of their two-minute songs seemed to be about the lead singer's car. The current song only seemed to have one lyric.

My Hyundai-die die die die die die!
My Hyundai-die die die die die!

The situation was so wrong in so many ways, B.J. didn't know where to begin. When he realized the Fire Pit was a biker bar, he'd begged Terry to let him stay on the Wünder-Bus. Just the sight of a ZZ Top beard was enough to make him tremble now. But Terry had promised all the parents that he'd keep the kids under his strict supervision at all times. He'd used some kind of Jedi mind trick to get them past the bouncer.

"Now listen, mate." Terry was yelling into B.J.'s ear as they leaned against the crowded bar. "The owner ain't gonna like you kids being here, so I need you to go along wif whatever I tell him, aw'ight?"

"What do you mean?"

"Just follow my lead," Terry said. "And don't *worry* so much. I know all these hard rockers look a bit dodgy, but these is some of the finest men and women in all of Philadelphia. Just follow my lead and you'll have a *blast* tonight!"

He wished Terry would stop using that word. Blast. It gave him terrible chills. Luckily, Layla was sitting next to him, squeezing his hand to keep him calm.

"Hey, Beej, do you smell that?" KeVonne was two stools down, digging his fingers into a bowl of stale cheddar goldfish.

"Smell what?"

"Bacon!" he replied with a smile of wonderment. Kev could smell bacon from three blocks away. It was on his Top Five Foods list, along with Pringles, Red Vines, glazed ham, and General Tso's chicken. "I think someone's cooking up some bacon, dude!"

"Shhh!" Terry shoved B.J. in the shoulder. "Tell your mate to shut it."

"Why? What's wrong?"

"*Mmmmmm.*" Kev shut his eyes. "It smells like Snausages, doesn't it? Beej, it's like I keep saying—why won't they make Snausages for people?"

"Zip it, Goggles!" Terry snapped. "Will you tell Bootsy to *zip* it?"

"Why?"

"Because that ain't bacon he's smelling. It's…"

"Me," a sickly voice declared. "He's smelling me. *Snort-snort-wheeeeeeeee.*"

B.J. had never heard a pig with laryngitis before. He had also never heard a man make such pig-like snorts and squeals. He was afraid to look up. He raised his head slowly—until he was staring straight into the beady eyes of the roly-poly Man-Pig standing behind the bar.

The Man-Pig's skin was as pink as a tulip, and his chest was as round as a Macy's Thanksgiving Day Parade float. He wore a bright white cowboy hat that cast a shadow over his pug nose and a red-checkered cowboy shirt—the front pockets of which were stretched so tightly over his sprawling man-boobs that the snaps wouldn't close.

Now that he was hovering so close, B.J. could finally smell it: the thick Snausage odor wafting from Man-Pig's tender pink baby skin. B.J. looked at the cowboy hat again, and that's when it hit him.

Oh my God…

"The Rodeo Pig!" B.J. and Layla mouthed the words almost simultaneously as they squeezed each other's hands. Who else could this giant canned ham in a square-dancing outfit possibly be? The book's prophecies were coming true so fast and furious now. It was hard to keep up.

"Don't be daft, Vince!" Terry laughed nervously, poking the Rodeo Pig in the stomach. "He ain't smelling *you*, mate. He's just smelling that delicious barbecue you're cookin' up out back!"

"Don't try to con me, Terry," Vince wheezed. "I know I smell like a roast pig. What I don't know is when my bar turned into a damn junior high. What's the deal bringing all these half-pints into my club? Get 'em outta here! *Snort-snort-wheeeeeeeeeee.*"

It wasn't actually a pig squeal at the end of Vince's sentences. It was more of a dry sinus whistle blowing through his blocked nasal passages every time he breathed in.

"Aw'ight, just chill, Vince," Terry said. "Don't have a pi—don't have a cow."

"Pig!" Vince spat. "You were gonna say 'Don't have a pig!'"

"Cow!" Terry insisted. "I was gonna say cow! And these ain't just any half-pints, Vince." Terry threw his arm around B.J.'s shoulder. "This here just happens to be my son, A.J."

What? Son? What? "It's B.J." B.J. murmured. *No, don't correct him, you idiot! You're supposed to follow his lead!*

Terry kicked him under the bar. "Yeah, that's right. This is my son A.J.B.J. He's just in from London, and I told his mum I'd look after him. Now how about four Cokes for my son and his mates, Vince?"

Vince grumbled something to himself. "Well, maybe I got some Cokes in the back *snort-snort.* But then they're *outta* here, Terry. You hear me? Out."

The moment Vince walked away, B.J. turned to Terry and dropped his poker face. "Are you *crazy*? Your *son*? How am I supposed to be your son?"

"Re-*lax*, man. It's all gonna work out."

"Uh, excuse me, folks," KeVonne nearly climbed over the bar to gain everyone's attention. "Is anyone going to tell me why that pink dude smells like he's made out of bacon?"

"Will you *pipe down*, Bootsy?" Terry signaled for Kev and the band to lean in closer as he lowered his voice. "Aw'ight, his name is Vince Moretti, but everyone calls him the Rodeo Pig. And he didn't always sound like that and he didn't always smell like that either, Goggles. Back in the day, Vince Moretti was as skinny as they come, and he had this *amazing* singing voice, Everyone thought he was going to be the next Jon Bon Jovi. Until one fateful night in New Jersey. Legend has it that somebody poisoned Vince wif hemrock."

"You mean hemlock?" Kev said.

"No, Goggles. Not hemlock. Hem*rock*."

"What the heck is hemrock?"

"You hear stories about it on tour," Terry said. "They say it's this nasty concoction wif a faint pork-like odor, and it's just like drinking battery acid. They say it'll burn your throat for life and leave you wif nothing but an undying thirst for bacon. Vince Moretti never sang another note in his life. And now he eats so much bacon that it's coming out of his pores, twenty-four-seven, which is why—Shhhh! He's coming back."

"All right, four Cokes," Vince grumbled, slamming them down on the bar. "Drink up and then the kids hit the road."

"Yeah, aw'ight, Vince," Terry smiled. "But you ain't gonna want 'em to go when I tell you my little secret."

"Oh yeah, what's that?"

Terry pulled Vince in closer. "Well, it just so happens, my son A.J.B.J. here is somefing of a musical genius. You gotta hear him *play*, Vince. His band is the genuine article. They're called the Good Supreme. Let 'em play just one tune tonight, aw'ight?"

B.J. spat half his Coke back into the glass. "*Say what?*"

Terry gave him a fatherly slap on the back. "Oh, don't be modest, A.J.B.J. You know you guys rock the house. And don't be so impolite, son. You ain't even given my buddy Vince here a proper London greeting."

A proper London…? Wait, now I'm supposed to be British? I don't know any British!

B.J.'s tongue was going numb again. "Uh…G'day, mate. I don't smell any bacon, but I'd love anothah shrimp on the bah-bee."

"You ain't *Australian*," Terry whispered, jabbing B.J. in the elbow.

Vince examined B.J. suspiciously. "You really Terry's son? 'Cause I don't see the family resemblance."

"Yeah, well, his mum's very Jewish," Terry explained.

"That's not what I meant!" Vince snarled. "Ain't he a little *tall* to be your kid?"

"Ay! We can have normal-size kids, you know? There's no need to be rude, Vince!"

"Fine," Vince groaned. "But he ain't playing my club, Terry. I let those Jonas kids play here once. They sang some tune about pirates, and all the bikers thought they were stealing your act, and they went ballistic. Things got ugly, man. I don't need another fight in my bar."

"Yeah, but this is totally different," Terry said. "The Good Supreme ain't from the glee club, mate. They play *real* rock music."

"Uh, Dad..." B.J. made another tragic attempt at an English accent. "We really dawn't need to play to-*noight.* We ain't even got our instruments."

"Oh, we got plenty of equipment on the Wünder-Bus, son."

"But..."

"It ain't gonna happen, Terry!" Vince's ravaged vocal cords were getting hoarser by the second. "There ain't nothin' you can say to change my mind."

Terry flashed a confident grin. "Well, I know there ain't nuffin' I can *say*, Vince. But I do think I have something that might change your mind."

Terry reached down to the sawdust-covered floor and lifted a small red Igloo cooler onto the bar. B.J. hadn't even noticed him carry it in. Now all their eyes were fixed on the cooler like it was some sort of holy relic. What did he have in that cooler that could possibly change the Rodeo Pig's mind? The possibilities were kind of disturbing. But Terry slid open the cooler and lifted out the answer.

It was a thick, maroon-colored slab of raw bacon.

Terry dangled the slab under Vince's pug nose.

"Oh dear Lord," Vince breathed. His anger drained away as his eyes zeroed in on the bacon. He hunched over slightly, and his fingers curled into pudgy little claws, fluttering along the meat's fatty white edges like he'd just found gold. He began to sniff and snort and wheeze and lick his tiny, puckered lips. "Oh dear Lord. It's Norwegian, isn't it? *Mmm-snort-snort wheeeeeee.* No, wait. *Snort-snort-snort.* Finland. Oh dear Lord. This is Finnish bacon."

"Organic farm in Helsinki," Terry said, grinning. "I know Finnish is your favorite, Vince."

Vince grabbed for the bacon, but Terry snapped it away.

"Ay! Do we have a deal? One tune for my boy and his mates?"

"One tune," Vince agreed. "One tune." He snatched the meat back from Terry's hands and cradled it in his arms like a child.

"Aw'ight!" Terry clapped his hands together. "Come on, A.J.B.J. Let's go get some gear from the bus, son. It's time these good people got a taste of the Good Supreme!"

"No, wait a second!" B.J. could feel a wave of panic setting in. Why was Terry doing this to him? Why hadn't he warned him first? "No, Terry, we're not ready to…Just, *no.*"

B.J. hopped off his barstool and took off through the sea of leather shoulders, dodging a minefield of studded bracelets as he searched the dark walls for glowing red exit signs.

★ ★ ★

"Hey, hold up, Levine!"

B.J. had figured that Layla or Kev might chase after him, but he hadn't expected Jann. Not in a million years.

"Where do you think you're going?" Jann pulled him into a dark corner and pushed him up against a crimson wall covered from floor to ceiling with motorcycle handlebars mounted like elk antlers.

"I can't do this," B.J. said, trapped between two handlebars. "I can't sing in front of these people, Jann. I thought I could keep doing this, but I can't."

"Keep doing what? What are you talking about?"

"It doesn't matter. You were right. These bikers hate my guts. You heard that Jonas Brothers story. They'll tear me apart. We gotta get out of here. We need to go home."

"No," Jann said. "No, we need to get up on that stage and play, dude."

"What? I thought you wanted to go home more than any of us!"

"Okay, maybe I was a little freaked when the bikers attacked, but I just panicked, dude. I mean, I'd just murdered Lola, you know…I was upset. But look where we are now. Look at this club. This place is *awesome*."

"Awesome? This place is a nightmare!"

"No, this place is *real*, Levine."

"What do you mean real?"

Jann stepped closer, making sure no one was close enough to overhear. "Look, do you remember what you said to me after the Tweetles show in the park? You said I should be making my money playing guitar, not making balloon animals for whiny kids, right?"

"I did?"

"Well, you were right. Just because I'm ridiculously good looking and wear awesome rocker clothes doesn't mean I'm legit. *This* place is legit. If I want to be in a real band, then I've got to play in a place like this. And the truth is..." His voice grew even softer now. "I didn't forget your song."

"Wait. Say that again?"

"I didn't forget your song, all right? I just didn't have the guts to play it for the D.O.G. I choked, dude. We all did. But not you. You wouldn't let anybody stop you. *That's* what a real rocker does. *That's* how you get a break. We *have* to play for these guys. Playing at some nasty club in Philly for a bunch of bikers who might hate us so much that they actually try to kill us? *That's* how you become a real band, Levine."

"Hey..."

"What?"

"You're not calling me Dockers anymore."

"Yeah," Jann said. "It doesn't really fit you anymore."

KeVonne and Layla burst through the wall of bikers, nearly falling against the handlebars.

"You guys better not be leaving," Kev said, "because we're going to load in some gear and play this gig right now. Don't tell me you're not down, Jann. The Fire Pit? You got to be down."

"I'm down," Jann said. "We should play 'Atlantic City.'"

"I thought you forgot it?" Kev said.

"Yeah, well, me and Levine just went over it, and I remember now."

"Awesome!" Layla grinned. "I want to play it too. Only one thing."

"What?"

"I want to add the 'hoo-hoo' part from '911 Emergency Toast.' We can stay on the G after the chorus and it'll totally fit."

"Why are you so obsessed with that 'hoo-hoo' part?" B.J. asked.

"I don't know," she said. "There's just something about it. It goes in or I don't play." She crossed her arms.

"Fine, it's in. No big!" Kev said. "Now let's move, people. I don't know when we became 'the Good Supreme,' but I like it. Let's bust out the jammy-jams. Hands in, y'all. Supreme on three. One, two, three…"

"*SUPREME!*"

The spotlight was so hot on his skin. The crowd was so quiet he could hear the Rodeo Pig wheezing. B.J.'s mouth was pressed to the microphone, his eyes fixed on the demon hordes that made up the Fire Pit's biker audience. The enthusiastic battle cry of "Supreme!" had only been five minutes ago, but it felt like a distant memory.

He'd thought it would be dark enough that he wouldn't have to see their faces, but it was just the opposite. The stage lights cast a creepy red glow on every single bearded face, their expressions ranging from bafflement to pure evil. B.J. could already see the headline:

SEVENTH-GRADER MURDERED ON STAGE BY
BEARDED BIKERS AND WOMEN WITH BAD PERMS

"What's with the *kid*, Vince?" a voice hollered.

"Yeah, is this a joke?" another voice laughed.

B.J. was beyond P.M.s now. This was something else. Something much more terrifying in the pit of his chest. It was the desperate wish for his mother to appear at the back of the club, march up to the stage, throw him over her shoulder, and whisk him away. But Mommy couldn't save him now.

"Um…Hi," he croaked into the mic. A piercing dose of feedback swallowed the entire room as the crowd covered their ears and flinched. "Sorry," he said. "Hi."

The next sound was like a mooing cow, which he soon realized was not a "moo" but a "boo." It launched a chain reaction of boos until the entire cavernous Fire Pit sounded like a pasture full of disgruntled cows. Pretty soon, there were hisses and squawks and growls. The entire farm had gone mad.

"Okay, ha ha, Vince!" one of the leather ogres shouted. "Very funny! Can we get a real band on stage here?"

The rest of the cows could not agree more and who was B.J. to argue? They were right. It was time for him to hit the road and let a real band take the stage.

"Thank you," he mumbled into the mic. He turned himself around and began his long walk off the stage, avoiding the disappointed stares of Jann, Layla, and KeVonne.

He'd almost made it to safety when he bumped into Terry's strong little hands.

"Ay! Get back up there, ya plonker!" Terry turned B.J. around and pushed his butt all the way back to the microphone. He reached up and pulled the mic stand down to his level.

"Listen up, fools!" Terry bellowed.

The moment they saw Terry, they began to cheer. "Terry! Terry! Terry!"

"Play a song, Terry! Where are the pirates, brother?"

"Yeah, aw'ight, keep your chaps on, mate!" Terry shouted back. "Everyone SHUT IT!"

The farm went silent.

"I *am* gonna sing a song," Terry said, his voice bathed in reverb. "I'm gonna sing a song with my boy here, who has flown in all the way from the UK to entertain you pathetic *hogs*. A-one-two-three-four..."

That was it. That was all the warning B.J. got. Jann grinned and ripped into the opening chords of "Atlantic City." KeVonne laced in some bass, and Layla the Whala was hammering away before B.J. could say a word.

"Now, give these fools a proper English greeting, son!" Terry shoved the mic back in B.J.'s hands, and grabbed a mic of his own.

"Uh...G'day mates!" B.J. screamed as the music blared.

"*YEEAAAAAHHHHH!*" the crowd hollered.

"That's *Australian*, ya tall plonker!" Terry screamed.

"*YEEEAAAAHHHHH!*" the crowd roared.

"Well, then, HOWDY, ya PLONKERS!" B.J. howled.

"*YEEEEAAAAHHHH!*"

What B.J. had failed to understand was the power of screaming insults. If you screamed at bikers and insulted them, they cheered. Who knew?

He jumped into the first verse before they could change their minds.

Shook off the sweat, shook the fog from my head
It wasn't night, wasn't morning, just a ditch in the empty bed

Don't know the day or the city I'm in
Another hotel, motel, Holiday Inn...

The burly bikers began to dance, which for them consisted mostly of bending their knees and holding their ladies' hands while the ladies danced. But still, there was no denying it. The demons were dancing! They *liked* the song.

As he neared the chorus, he began to hear faint screaming from behind him. He peered back and saw Layla, beads of sweat flying off her head as she banged out the backbeat. She was shouting something he couldn't make out, as he was too busy trying to sing.

"The tutu!" she was saying.

He tried to lean his ear closer as the stage rumbled beneath his feet.

"The hoo-hoo!" Jann shouted into B.J.'s ear.

Right. She wants the hoo-hoo part after the chorus. He gave a big nod and made sure Kev was on board.

When they hit the chorus, he could feel the energy in the room jump to another gear. The bikers thrust their devil horns high in the air and risked serious whiplash with a burst of joyful head-banging—somehow miraculously keeping their bandannas on the entire time.

He couldn't believe it. He had earned their devil horns. It was one thing to get the devil horns from a bunch of middle-aged

D.O.G. fans but to get them from a horde of genuine bikers? That was the ultimate honor.

She took the money all night
She took the money all right
She took the money from my pocket and she turned out the light
She left my blood on the road
She took the love of my life
She took the money, yeah, all night
Hoo hoo HOO hoo-hoo
Hoo hoo HOO hoo-hoo…

And when he began to "hoo-hoo," something truly remarkable happened.

They began to sing along. All of them. Every man and woman in the club—even Terry and the rest of the band onstage.

The pirates had pushed through to the front of the crowd, swinging their arms and hoo-hooing just as if they were yo-ho-hoing an old pirate shanty. Terry pulled his mic from its stand and hoo-hooed at the top of his lungs, bouncing up and down as if the entire stage were a trampoline. Even Vince, the Rodeo Pig, who surely wasn't singing much more than a sickly "oink," was hoo-hooing.

B.J. finally understood Layla's obsession with the hoo-hoo. It was so gloriously simple that anyone could sing it. There were no words to worry about. No complicated melody to learn. You could sing it instantly—whether you knew the song or not. And that, B.J. realized, was rock and roll gold.

B.J. wasn't much more than a shameless copycat. But Layla? Layla was a musical genius. She understood the raw, irresistible power of the hoo-hoo.

Hoo-hoo-HOO-hoo-hoo
Hoo-hoo-HOO-hoo-hoo...

★ ★ ★

The next few minutes were so fuzzy, Sammy.

I remember standing alone in this big room backstage. I ran back there while my band was breaking down and Terry and the Pirates were setting up. I didn't run away because I was scared or because I was having a Panic Moment. I just had to be alone for a minute.

You probably know this, but when you stand in a spotlight, feeling like you're about to die, and you sing a song for a hundred angry bikers and they actually <u>like</u> it, it's basically impossible to keep your cool afterward. You turn into a big, corny, hyped-up mess. My heart was racing so fast, I thought I might have a heart attack. Plus, it was so unbelievably hot and bacony. The smell of organic Finnish bacon was everywhere.

Everything felt so huge. I felt like I was ready to play stadiums and tour the world and pose for the cover of Rolling Stone. I felt like the Good Supreme had just become a part of Fire Pit history. That's why I was looking at all the pictures on the walls.

The backstage room was covered with pictures of bands. There was a plaque by the ceiling that read "THE FIRE PIT WALL OF FLAME." It seemed like all the '80s rock bands in the world had played the Fire Pit: Whitesnake and Skid Row and ZZ Top and Poison and Motley Crue. Even Mr. Bon Jovi had played there! I was thinking about him when I started to hear the music.

At first, I thought the music was in my head. This beautiful acoustic guitar, strumming these amazing harmonies. I thought it was one of those moments of clarity Dad talked about when you start to hear a new song forming in your brain. Divine inspiration, Dad calls it. But then I realized that it was coming from somewhere else backstage.

I started to follow the beautiful sound down a narrow hallway. At first, it was just this guitar strumming, but then I heard a voice singing. I think it was maybe the prettiest voice I've ever heard. She sounded young and cool, but she also sounded kind of sad in a way, which only made it prettier. And then I turned a corner and I finally found her. But I didn't tell her I'd found her yet because I wanted to hear what she was singing.

★ ★ ★

Somewhere I don't know
That's where I'm going
The road goes on and on
Oh, I don't care, but I do
Oh, I don't care but I...but I'll get away from you
Sooner or later
I'll float away from here too
And I know that once you're all alone
The shame will be on YOU.

YOU. YOU...

"Hey!" She dropped her guitar to her knees when she saw B.J. Her composition notebook fell to the floor and her pale cheeks went pink. "How long have you been standing there, jerk?"

He was too busy looking at her to answer. From the sound of her voice, he'd expected to find a grown woman in her twenties, but she was just a girl. Probably around the same age as he was—definitely no older than fifteen. Her long platinum blond hair dipped down behind her back, except for two long braids that framed her slim face. Her T-shirt was such a bright shade of orange that she seemed to glow like a campfire.

The braids fell over her eyes as she leaned from the battered couch to pick up her notebook. "Hello? I said how long have you been standing there?"

The problem was this: There were certain girls who were just too pretty to talk to. So pretty that B.J. felt compelled to leave the cramped little room immediately.

"Wait…" She took a closer look at his face. "Wait, it's *you.* You're the British kid! That was your song!" Her cheeks perked up into a gorgeous smile.

Just when he'd almost opened his mouth to speak, she'd reminded him that he was supposed to be the "British kid." *Oh, dude, no, no, no. Not the British kid.*

But maybe that wasn't such a bad thing. If the real B.J. Levine couldn't talk to this girl, then maybe the British kid could.

"Yeh," B.J. said, desperately searching for a decent British accent. "Oym the British kid."

"Dude, I *loved* your song," she said. "What's your name?" She reached out for a shake.

Do NOT say B.J. Levine. The British kid is not named B.J. Levine. Say something cool and rockin' and British.

"I'm Nigel," he said. "Nigel 'Hot Wings' Thunderdome."

She cocked her head to the side. "Wow," she laughed. "That's a serious name."

"Yeah, well, moy dad's a very serious guy."

"Yeah, so is mine." The smile fell from her face, but she brought it back in a heartbeat. "Hey, I've played in London a few times. Which part of England are you from?"

"Which part…?"

"Yeah, not London, right? You have a different accent."

"Roight, not London…" *Oh, dude, what's another part of England? Say something!* "Hillshire Farms," he said. "I'm from Hillshire Farms, England."

"Oh. Never heard of it."

That's because it's a breakfast sausage.

"Well, it's an honor to meet you, Nigel. I'm Sammy."

B.J. smiled. "Sammy. Is dat short for Samantha?"

"No, it's short for Sambora. You know, like Richie Sambora from Bon Jovi? My dad is kind of obsessed with Bon Jovi."

"No *way*. So is mine!"

"Really? I didn't think the Brits were so into Jovi."

"Oh, yeah, well, my dad is kind of odd. I mean, he's very odd."

"So is *mine*," she laughed. "God, I think we have the same dad, Nigel."

"Yeh," he laughed. He sat down on the opposite edge of the couch, trying not to stare at her. "Sammy, dat song you were just playing. Dat was lovely."

British people say "lovely," right? Or did I just sound like the biggest wuss on the planet?

"Ugh, no it's wasn't," she moaned. "That's not even a song

yet. I can't believe you heard that. Ugh, I'm so embarrassed." She covered her beautiful eyes. "Nigel, if I tell you something, do you swear you won't laugh?"

"I swear," he said.

"Okay. I loved your 'hoo-hoo' song so much that I ran back here and I was trying to write something just as good. How lame is that?"

"It's not lame. Not at awl."

"It's lame." She covered her eyes again.

B.J. couldn't understand it, but every time she covered her eyes, there was something about her. Something so familiar. He was sure he'd never met her before because if he had, there was no way on Earth he would have forgotten. But why was she so familiar? Why did it feel like he already knew her?

"Can I tell you something even lamer, Nigel?" she asked.

"What?"

"It's about your song. I know how corny this sounds, but I felt like your song was about me."

"About you? Did you steal all of some bloke's money in Atlantic City?"

"*No*," she laughed. "It's just this stupid nickname my dad has for me. My dad calls me 'the Money.' Like, instead of calling me 'honey,' he calls me 'Money.'"

"Why?"

"No, it's stupid. Forget it."

"No, tell me why."

The patter of rubber sneakers came squeaking down the hallway before Sammy could answer.

"Where *are* you?" Layla's voice was calling from down the hall. "That was amazing, Levine! What did I tell you about the hoo-hoo? What did I tell you? Where are you? Ah, there you are!" She leaped into the cramped little backstage room, poised to jump B.J. for a celebratory hug. But just as she threw open her arms, she saw Sammy glowing like a bright orange flame in the corner of the couch.

Layla stumbled to a halt. She was panting with excitement, but her smile faded as her eyes drifted from Sammy's perfect face to B.J.'s and then back to Sammy's.

"Who are you?" Layla asked rudely.

"I'm Sammy," she smiled, putting out her hand for a shake.

Layla didn't shake her hand. "Sammy who?"

"Uh..." Sammy let her hand drop back on her guitar. "Sammy Springstein."

Layla's eyes widened. "Springsteen like *Springsteen*?"

"No," Sammy sighed. "No, it's Springstein with an *I*. It's a long story."

"Oh." Layla turned back to B.J. "What are you doing back here? What, do you have groupies already?"

Why did he suddenly feel like he'd done something wrong? "No, we were just...I mean...Sammy was just telling me..."

An even louder storm of footsteps came shuffling down the hall before he could finish his sentence. Now it was a host of heavy boots—everything from Bootsy Boots to biker boots. The next thing he knew, the tiny backstage room was filling up with the rest of the Good Supreme, followed by a trail of hulking, giddy bikers. He didn't even know there was such a thing as giddy bikers.

"There he is!" one of the bikers shouted. He looked a little like one of the B.L.A.S.T. crew, but he was younger—closer to B.J.'s parents' age, which made him a little less frightening. "Come here, you gangly freak! You rocked my world, man!" He hoisted B.J. up off the floor and crushed him in a painful bear hug.

"Get off of me, fatso!" B.J. shouted. He was finally learning to speak Biker.

"AH-HAHAHAHAH!" the biker guffawed. He dropped B.J. back to his feet. "That *song*, brother! I loved that *song*! You took me all the way *back*! I felt like I was right back at a Bayonette show in '97, man! How'd you do that?"

"Bayonette? Who's Bayonette?" B.J. asked.

"*Who's* Bayonette?" The biker shook B.J. like a rag doll. "Shut up, kid. Don't tell me you weren't listening to tons of Bayonette when you wrote that song. You must have found some of their CDs back in England or something."

"No," B.J. said, trying to remember his British accent. "I don't know nuffin' about this Bayonette, mate."

"Bayonette was my dad's old band," Sammy said. "Oh my God, Nigel. You did sound just like Bayonette."

The room was filling up with so many bikers that B.J. couldn't see Sammy's face anymore.

"Come *on*," the biker complained. "*Bayonette.* They were the gods of Bayonne."

"Bayonne?" B.J. felt a cold chill. Albino Paulie had used that word at the station. *You just had to find your inner Bayonne...* "What's Bayonne?" B.J. asked.

"New *Jersey.*" The biker looked heartily offended. "Bayonne, New Jersey. Man, don't they teach New Jersey in England? *Bayonette* was gonna be the next Bon Jovi. They played the Fire Pit all the time." He yanked B.J. through the jam-packed room till they were nearly up against the wall. "There. Right there. That's Bayonette, brother."

A hundred Wall of Flame photos were plastered across the wall, but as far as B.J. was concerned, there was only one. The biker's finger was pointing at an old photo of another hair band. But it was the face under all that hair that made it stand out.

Dad?

Is that my dad?

There was no question. Half of his long blond hair was teased out six inches from his head and the other half was covering most of his face, but his features were unmistakable. It was Jason "Hot Wings" Levine with the face of a twenty-year-old boy. He was doing the classic windmill on his electric guitar, which was shaped like a bayonet rifle. There were three other dudes in the band, but the drummer and the bass player had so much hair that B.J. couldn't see them. The only other face he could see was the lead singer's, and he was one scary looking kid.

The lead singer of Bayonette had super-sharp cheekbones, wide-open crazy eyes, a big hooked nose, jet-black hair spiked out like Medusa's, and a long black leather coat down to his ankles. He was raising a big, jewel-encrusted goblet to the camera with one hand, and flashing the devil horns with the other.

"Who's that dude?" B.J. asked.

"Who's that dude?" The biker couldn't believe his ears. "Are you serious? Kid, you really don't know anything about Jersey rock history, do you? That's the Overlord, man."

The Overlord? My dad was in a band with the OVERLORD?

"Hey, Sammy!" A cruel, booming voice suddenly silenced the room.

B.J. turned around and peered over all the bikers' shoulders at the tall, slim wraith of a man standing in the doorway, shrouded in a long black leather coat.

It was like jumping through an instant time warp. B.J. was staring at the same kid he'd just seen in the old picture on the wall—the same wild eyes, the same sharp cheekbones, the same black Medusa hair—only now he'd aged twenty years. His smooth, boyish skin had turned into grizzled-black stubble and a goatee, but it was the same face.

The Overlord. B.J. was trapped in an eight-foot square room with the Overlord.

"Where is Sammy?" he demanded. "Where is she?"

"I'm right here, Dad," Sammy sighed as she stood up off the couch.

Dad? Did she just say "Dad"?

"I've been looking *all over* for you," the Overlord complained. "Pack up your gear, Money. We're leaving right now."

"What? Why?" Sammy glanced across the room at B.J. He could see that same sadness in her eyes that he'd heard in her singing voice. "We can't leave now, Dad. We haven't even played our set yet."

Their set? She's in a band with him?

"Now means *now*," the Overlord snapped. "I just canceled the set."

"Why?"

"Never mind *why*. Just get your stuff! *Move*, Money. This ain't a democracy!"

There was nothing more horrible than the sound of a father yelling at his daughter. It was so much worse than the sound of a father ignoring his son. The bikers were all trying to avoid the tension by staring down at the dirty gray carpet.

"But I can't go yet," Sammy said. "I'm still talking to Nigel."

"Nigel? Who's Nigel?"

The Overlord scanned the room, his eyes shifting rapidly from an angry simmer to a full-on raging boil. B.J. tried to melt into the Wall of Flame. He clenched his fists and prayed for the power of invisibility, but it was no use.

Their eyes locked. The Overlord fixed his sights on B.J. like a cruel hunter finding a defenseless fawn. B.J. could feel the weight of his gaze crushing him to the ground.

"Nigel," he murmured. "Let me make something very clear to you, Nigel. You will not speak to my daughter again. If you attempt to speak to my daughter again, there will be consequences."

"Dad!" Sammy tried to interrupt him, but he raised one long finger and silenced her instantly.

"Do you understand what I'm saying to you, Nigel? Consequences."

"Yes, sir," B.J. replied. He wanted to look at Sammy, but that didn't seem like the best idea just now.

"Good," the Overlord said. He turned to Sammy. "Pack up, and get your butt on the bus. *Now.* I'm getting my goblet and we're leaving."

B.J. could see Sammy's eyes growing moist with tears, though she was trying to hide it.

"Fine," she said, her voice quavering. "It'll take me a minute, all right?"

"*One* minute," her father replied. He gave B.J. one last death glare and marched out the door, his leather coattails flapping in his wake.

The room stayed deathly silent as Sammy struggled to get her guitar back in its case and sling it over her shoulder. She picked up her composition notebook, scrawled something down quickly, ripped out the page, and folded it.

She swiped her arm across her eye to capture one escaped tear. "Will you please pass this to Nigel?" She handed Layla the folded paper, glanced at B.J. for less than a second, and then was gone.

Layla stared at the folded-up paper. She was obviously dying to read it, but she honored Sammy's request, passing it to Jann, who passed it to Kev, who passed it from biker to biker until it landed in B.J.'s hands. He opened it up.

> *Help me, Nigel. I'm his rock and roll hostage. Please come find me at the gauntlet. Do NOT show anyone this note.*

"What does it say?" Layla asked.

"It's nothing," B.J. said. "I just asked her for the lyrics to one of her songs."

Jann and Kev were all smiles as they jumped back aboard the Wünder-Bus. They had taken the Fire Pit by storm.

"Well, mates!" Terry wrapped his arm around Jann's waist. "It's been quite a noight! But I suppose it's just about time to take you kids home, ay?"

"*Nooooo,*" Jann and Kev groaned in unison.

"I know. I know." Terry grinned. "It's a bloody shame. What a tour this would be! Terry and the Pirates and the Good Supreme. A double bill to rock your faces to the ground!"

"Yo-ho!" the Pirates cheered.

"Come on, Terry," Jann said. "Let's do one more gig before we head home, dude. One more gig."

"Yeah!" Kev agreed. "We're on a roll tonight. We're on *fuego*!"

"Aw, I'd love to, Goggles, but I promised your folks I'd get ya back tonight—safe and sound. Besides, me and the pirates gotta get some sleep tonight 'cause we got somefing real big tomorrow. I'm afraid it's closing time, mates."

"*Boooooo.*" Kev and Jann knocked shoulders and frowned.

"I know it." Terry smiled sadly, patting them both on the back. "But what's roight is roight. Just ask your fearless leader here. Tell 'em, A.J.B.J. Tell 'em the fun's over and it's time to head home."

B.J. had practically forgotten his glorious rock and roll moment already. All he could think about was that shocking photo of his mega-haired father from a completely different life. And the even more shocking image of the Overlord standing next to his father, raising his jewel-encrusted goblet to the skies.

And Sammy, glowing in her bright orange T-shirt, trapped on a bus with her father.

"A.J.B.J.?" Terry searched B.J.'s eyes for signs of life. "You in there, li'l big man? Tell your mates you've gotta go home."

"No," B.J. said. "We're not going home yet. We're going to the Gauntlet."

Terry grinned with amazement. "Bloody hell...How did you know we was going to the Gauntlet?"

"What's the Gauntlet?" Kev asked.

Layla turned to B.J. She'd seemed a little quiet since meeting Sammy, but now her somber expression began to melt away as a glowing smile took its place.

"Chapter 5," she whispered. "You're going all the way."

"All the way," B.J. said.

CHAPTER ten

The Legend of the Good Supreme

Chapter 5

His Trials Were Many and Mighty, But He Knew There Was Only One Way Back Home. He Had to Find His Sacred Pinky, Confront the Overlord, and Win the Gauntlet. Then and Only Then Would He Become the Good Supreme…

The Gauntlet. What is it, mates? Well, as I explained to young Goggles last night, it is only the biggest rock and roll competition in the entire tristate area."

Terry was pacing up and down the aisle of the Wünder-Bus like a little general readying his troops for their toughest mission. He'd changed into black spandex pants and replaced his lavender silk scarf with an indigo silk scarf. The afternoon sun was blaring through the windows.

"This competition is so bloody huge," Terry went on, "it is a battle of such *Olympic* proportions dat it only happens once every five years."

Five years...

B.J. flashed back to an image of Merv standing at his doorway.

"*Five years!*" he was shouting, pointing his finger at Dad. "*This has to happen now, Hot Wings! You know it, and I know it, and everybody else knows it!*"

B.J. shook it off just as he'd shaken off so many thoughts today, especially the sound of his mother screaming in his ear when he told her they'd be arriving in New York a day later than planned.

He'd told her that the bus had broken down and that they couldn't get it fixed until the next day and that Terry had put them up in a nice hotel for the night, none of which was true. Lying had become second nature by this point.

Dad hadn't gotten on the phone once. Was he even worried? That was another thought to shake off as B.J. tried to stay focused on Terry's sermon.

"Bands from all across the East Coast gather here to do battle," Terry said. "They come from *all* over for the grand prize of *twenty-five thousand* U.S. dollars."

"Twenty-five Gs?" Jann was salivating.

"Yeh, but it ain't about the money, Jann. These artists ain't coming to the Holy Land for cash. They're coming to the Holy Land for the title, mate. They're coming to be crowned the one and only MEGALORD OF RRRROCK!"

"Okay, where *is* the Holy Land?" Layla asked.

Terry shook his head with disappointment. "My God. The American education system really is a shambles, ain't it? The Holy Land is only the bloody birthplace of working-class rock and roll. It's only the blessed, hallowed ground where Bruce Springsteen and the E Street band first made their name—where Jon Bon Jovi was first shot through the heart and rocked his first face. The *Holy Land*, darlin'. Asbury Park, New Jersey." He spread his arms out to the windows. "Forget all that crap you've seen on MTV, mates. *This* is the Jersey Shore."

B.J. slid open his window. Now he could see patches of beach just a few blocks beyond the road. He could smell the salty combination of sewage and seawater. He could see brightly painted signs splashed across a huge, dilapidated building that looked kind of like an old castle.

WELCOME TO ASBURY PARK!

WELCOME TO THE BOARDWALK!

"Now, the Gauntlet does have a few rules." Terry held up a finger for each rule. "Rule One: You only get to play one song. They got too many bands to judge a whole set. Rule Two: You gotta play an original song—no covers. And Rule Three:

You can only play in one band. They can't have a bunch of blokes forming five different bands to try and haul in all the cash.

"The bands have already been playing for the last three days. Tonight's the last night of the competition, but I called in a few favors and I got us both a slot for this evening. And I will admit, I got a good feeling about this year, mates. I don't care if it's Terry and the Pirates or the Good Supreme. I think one of us has got a real shot at taking down the reigning Megalord."

"Who's the reigning Megalord?" B.J. asked. But some part of him knew the answer before he'd even asked.

"I believe you've all just met him," Terry said. His expression grew very serious. "Damian 'The Overlord' Springstein."

"Springsteen like *Springsteen*?" Jann squawked.

"No," Terry said. "He was born Damian Rifkowitz, but he legally changed his name to Springstein with an I when he was sixteen. That's how insane he is. That's how obsessed he is wif New Jersey rock and roll. Plus, he's got his fourteen-year-old daughter playing the guitar, and that girl is a bloody prodigy. She's like Jeff Beck and Richie Sambora all rolled into one adorable little blond Kewpie doll. *She's* what's winning him all the competitions now. The judges can't resist her."

Layla frowned and sunk down deeper in her seat.

"Well, we can still beat 'em," KeVonne said. "We got Beej and

Layla and Jann Solo, dude! How they gonna deal with that?" He bumped fists with Jann.

"Yeah, but we've got to start rehearsing right away," Layla said. "We should just rehearse on the bus for the rest of the day, right, Levine?"

The Wünder-Bus was weaving its way past a caravan of tour buses. All B.J. could think about was which one might be Sammy's.

"Levine…?" Layla punched him in the arm.

"Yeah, right," he said. "Rehearse. Definitely. But I think I should go get us something to eat first."

"Now that is a good idea," Kev said. "I'm starting to smell burgers out there. Is anyone else smelling burgers?"

Kev was right. The tour buses had filled all the parking lots, turning Asbury Park into more of a trailer park, and the bands had already started firing up their tailgate barbecues.

"Pull over here, Graham!" B.J. jumped out of his seat and ran to the front of the bus.

"What?" Layla stood up. "Where are you going?"

"I just told you," B.J. said. "I'm going to go see if I can mooch us some burgers."

"But…"

"I'll be right back," B.J. promised. "You guys just find a good spot to park and I'll come find you."

With that, he leaped off the Wünder-Bus and started his search for Sammy.

★ ★ ★

Navigating the endless maze of buses was impossible. There was a new gang of skeevy-looking musicians at every turn. Long hair, short hair, shaved heads, tattoos, and piercings—all blurring together into a Circus of a Thousand Rockers.

They were all camped out by their little barbecue grills, roasting hot dogs, hoisting beers, and blasting mind-numbing power chords at each other—bus after bus, guitar after guitar, bad band name after bad band name. *The Dirty Shirts, Troubled Doctor, Destructicus, Icky Micky, No Elmo No Cry…*

How would he ever find Sammy, the beautiful needle in this greasy haystack?

But there was one way. He stopped looking and he started listening…

He closed his eyes and tried to listen through the din of fake Van Halen solos for the sounds of Sammy. If there was one thing he'd learned from his dad, it was that songwriters worked on the same song for days at a time—sometimes playing nothing more than the opening riff again and again until a good lyric hit them. He had only heard Sammy's song for twenty seconds at the Fire Pit, but it was permanently etched into his brain.

And sure enough, when he focused, he began to pick up that unearthly lilt in her voice.

Sooner or later
I'll float away from here too
And I know that once you're all alone
The shame will be on YOU.
YOU. YOU…

He began to follow the voice, weaving his way through buses, burgers, and beers until he finally saw her yellow-gold hair and her bright orange hoodie reflecting the afternoon sun. She was sitting in a little turquoise foldout camping chair on the pavement, hunched over her acoustic guitar. She was so focused on the guitar that she didn't notice him at first, but when she looked up, her face was overcome by emotions that he couldn't read. Whether it was joy or relief or just pure disbelief, B.J. knew one thing for sure: Sammy hadn't expected to see him again. She hadn't thought he would actually come find her.

"Nigel? Oh my *God!*" She laid her guitar gently on the pavement and took off toward him, but she stopped just short of hugging him, leaving them standing awkwardly, face-to-face. "You found me." She clasped her hands together, bobbing in place, her long golden braids swinging across her gray-green eyes.

"Well, I had to," B.J. said. "I mean…" He lowered his voice to a whisper and tried to remember his dismal British accent. "You said you was in a hostage situation."

"I am, Nigel," she whispered, flicking her eyes to the left and then the right as if someone might be watching. "It's really bad."

"Well, Oym here to help," he said.

"Come sit with me."

She grabbed the sleeve of B.J.'s T-shirt and dragged him back toward her foldout camping chair.

"Look, I have to explain it quick, all right? He won't be gone for too much longer. He never leaves me alone for too long because he thinks I might try to run away. And I don't know why, but he *totally* hates your guts, Nigel. Not like normal 'Don't talk to boys' stuff.' I mean he straight-up *hates* you. Like if he caught me talking to you right now, I think he'd literally try to rip your face off."

B.J. felt a dry, scratchy lump growing inside his throat. "But why?" His voice cracked on his first attempt to speak. "Why does he hate me so much? He doesn't even know me."

"I don't know," Sammy said. "But it doesn't matter, Nigel, because we're going to be long gone before he figures us out."

"Gone where?"

"To California," she said. "I'm pretty sure that's where my mom is. Either California or Poland."

B.J. was getting more confused, and Sammy could tell.

"Okay, I'm sorry," she said. "I told you I had to go fast."

"Maybe just a *little* slower?"

"Okay. A little slower," she agreed. "Nigel, what I'm about to tell you is not something I tell everybody. I'm only telling you because I trust you and because I need you."

"You do?" It was so strange listening to Sammy talk. She was only a year older, but she talked like a nearly full-grown adult.

"I do," she said. "I need you, Nigel. So just listen, okay?"

"Okay."

"I've been a tour baby my whole life," Sammy said. "My mom and dad were in a band together, and they'd take me with them everywhere—every hotel, every motel—and there was even a little crib in the back of their old van. I mean, I don't remember most of it because I was only, like, a year old. I just have these bits and pieces, you know? Pictures in my head. But I swear I remember the night Dad took me away."

"Took you away?"

"My dad stole me, Nigel. He stole me from my mom. He snuck me out of a hotel one night, left my mom behind, and took me on the road for good. I can still picture his giant hands reaching down, pulling me away from my baby quilt, and throwing me into a car seat."

"But didn't your mum try to stop him?" B.J. asked, trying to stay British.

"I think she was asleep when he took me."

"But didn't she try to find you when she woke up?"

"I think she's *still* trying to find me. I know she is because there was this one time a few years ago when a desk guy at a motel tried to give me a note. He said it was from some chick named Astrid—and Astrid is my *mom's* name. But Dad came into the motel and snatched the note away before I could read it. He said it was for him. I watched him read it and then rip it up, and no matter how many times I asked him about it, he'd never talk about that note again. And from that day on, we *never* stayed in motels. Now we only travel on the Overlord tour bus. That bus is my house, Nigel. That's where I live."

"All the time?"

"*All* the time. I've been homeschooled on a tour bus. I live in a jail with wheels. He won't even let me have a computer or a cell phone. The only thing I can do all day is play guitar. How do you think I got so good at it? I got so good at the guitar that he put me in the band when I was twelve. Now we just travel around the world, playing all these competitions. And we always win, Nigel. The judges see this cute family band with this little blond girl wailing away on the solos, and they give us all the votes. But Dad keeps *all* the money. How am I supposed to get to California or Poland and find my mom if he won't let me have a dollar of my own? That's where you come in."

"Huh?"

Sammy grabbed hold of B.J.'s hands, pressing them urgently against the armrests of the camping chair. "Nigel, we need to form a secret band. A band that my dad doesn't know about."

"A secret band?"

"Yes. If he found out about it, then he'd just throw me back on the bus and we'd hit the road again. You're my *one* chance to escape."

"I don't understand. Why me?"

"What do you mean 'Why you?' Because you're so *good.* I haven't been able to stop thinking about your 'Atlantic City' song. You're such a good songwriter."

"No," B.J. mumbled. "No, I'm a lousy writer, Sammy. It's really just that one song..."

"Oh, don't be so insecure! Everywhere I go on tour, all I hear are these ultra-lame songs about 'rocking the night away' and 'making you mine' and blah, blah, blah. They don't get that if you want to be a real megalord of rock, you've gotta speak the *truth*, you know? You've gotta speak the Truth with a capital T. I'm still working on it, but *you*, Nigel, you get it. That song was so *real*, I could feel it. Dude, with your songwriting and singing and my guitar playing, there's no way we can lose. We can win the Gauntlet together, I *know* it. And then I'll finally have the money to get away from Dad and look for my mom."

B.J. couldn't help momentarily beaming with pride. He couldn't help thinking about how far he'd come in these last few strange and crazy days. What an amazing story it would be. Going all the way from Jann walking out on him in the basement to playing in a band with the über-rocking child prodigy Sammy Springstein!

But then he remembered the rules. Terry had made the strict rules of the Gauntlet abundantly clear. You were only allowed to compete in *one* band.

"But, Sammy..."

"What? What's wrong?" Her eyes crinkled with worry as she glimpsed around again for signs of her father.

"No, it's just...If I play with you, then I wouldn't be able to play with my band."

Sammy breathed an anxious sigh. "I know that, Nigel. I know. But you'll have the rest of your life to play with your band."

"But..."

"Nigel, can't you see this is destiny? We were *supposed* to meet. Look at all the weird stuff we have in common. You write songs that sound just like my dad's old band. Our dads are both freaks in the exact same way. They're both obsessed with New Jersey rock and they're both obsessed with Bon Jovi."

"That's true..."

"I bet if I hadn't been on the road my whole life, we would have met when we were little kids. Maybe at a Bon Jovi concert or at the Fire Pit. We'd probably *already* be in a band together. I mean, look at your T-shirt!" She tugged at the center of his father's black tee. "It's like Bon Jovi is talking to us right now, Nigel. 'We're halfway there…' That's you and me. We're halfway to winning the Gauntlet and changing our lives."

"You think?"

"I don't think, I *know*. I've always felt like Bon Jovi's songs were speaking straight to me. 'Keep the Faith.' That's what I've had to do my whole life, waiting for my mom to find me. 'She's a little runaway.' That's me on the run with my dad. 'It's my life—it's now or never.' That's right now, Nigel. If you won't play with me tonight, then I don't think I'll ever have another chance to get away. I'll never get back home. I feel just like Bon Jovi, walking those streets with that loaded six-string, never knowing if I'll make it back. I mean, sure, I've seen a million faces and I've rocked—"

"Okay, *hold on* just one second." B.J. grabbed her arm. "I got some *serious* questions about those lyrics. First of all, is he holding a gun or is it a guitar? Because there ain't no way to 'load' a guitar and a gun definitely ain't got six strings. But *way* more important, can you *please* tell me, just how exactly you rock a—?"

"Nigel, run," Sammy suddenly whispered.

"What?"

"Oh God, run now. *Run!*"

B.J. followed Sammy's eyes across the parking lot. A towering wraithlike figure was emerging from the shadows in a full-length leather coat and titanium-studded bracelets. His dark blue eyes were on fire with rage.

"*You!*" the Overlord growled, pointing his black-polished fingernail-claw at B.J. "What did I *tell* you about *staying away* from my *daughter*?"

"Good God," B.J. murmured as his spine went ice cold with terror. He shot up from the camping chair, nearly tripping on his own spindly legs. He clumsily backed away as the Overlord picked up speed.

"Sammy," B.J. croaked. "I think I've got to go."

"I know," Sammy said, rising quickly to her feet to stand between them. "*Go*," she whispered. "Just meet me back here in an hour—back behind that dumpster." She pointed furtively to a tie-dye painted dumpster at the edge of the lot—behind three other tour buses. "*Please*," she begged. "You've got to come back for me, Nigel. You're my only hope."

"*YOU!*" the Overlord howled. "*NIGEL! I said get away from her!*" He was closing in so quickly that his coat was rippling behind him like long black-feathered demon wings.

B.J. stumbled into a hundred-and-eighty-degree pivot and launched into a full-blown Forrest Gump dash, pumping his legs like two beanstalk pistons, not even daring to look back at that super-gelled jet-black Medusa hair catching up from behind.

He ducked into a narrow maze of closely parked tour buses, bouncing brutally off the bumpers like a human pinball until he finally saw a clear path through the boardwalk to the crowded Asbury Park beach.

You did it! he told himself, breathing in a massive whiff of the salty ocean. *I think you lost him!*

He risked a quick glimpse over his shoulder and grinned with sweet relief. Not one black leather coat in sight. But when he turned back to the boardwalk, he came crashing into a wall of wrinkly powder-white flesh.

"AAAAAAAAHHHHHHH!"

"Will you *shut it*, Scarecrow?"

Albino Paulie. Of course it was Albino Paulie. He'd nabbed B.J. by the elbows and pulled him back into an alley between a tattoo parlor and a french fry shack on the boardwalk.

Albino Paulie shoved B.J. up against the wall, covering his mouth with his calloused hand again. This was becoming an all-too-familiar dance. "One more girl-screech and they're gonna flatten you into a geek panini. *Comprende*, Scarecrow?"

"Not really," B.J. mumbled into Paulie's palm.

Being chased by the Overlord had been so terrifying that Albino Paulie seemed almost harmless by comparison. B.J. had practically expected to see Paulie again, given the way he kept popping up at every turn. His first instinct was to flail his arms until he broke free from Paulie's grip, but then he remembered one simple fact: Paulie had tried to *save* him from B.L.A.S.T. at the bus station. Paulie—despite looking like Gandalf's evil rocker twin—was actually one of the good guys.

"Why ain't you been heeding my *wawnings*, kid?" Paulie looked furious. "Are you *trying* to get yourself disappeared by these B.L.A.S.T. psychos?" Paulie's face was so close that B.J. could see his reflection in his dark wraparound shades.

"No." B.J. peeled Paulie's hand from his mouth. "I swear I'm not trying to do anything. I only came here because—"

"Because you're a stone-cold skinny fool?"

"No, because I met this—"

"Oh, I ain't *askin'*, Scarecrow. I'm *tellin'* you! You're only here 'cause you're a stone-cold skinny fool! Somehow, despite all my wawnings, you *still* don't seem to get that you're in grave danger right now. You're about ten minutes from being blasted, kid. *B.L.A.S.T.*-ed into a thousand little scarecrow pieces."

"But I just got away from him," B.J. argued.

"Ah, *jeez with cheese!*" Paulie shook his black-gloved hands in frustration. "How else can I spell this out for you? Didn't I tell you that B.L.A.S.T. was trying to take you down?"

"Yeah, but..."

"What, do I need to be more specific?"

"No, it's not that...Well, actually, yes, if you could be a little more specific that might help."

"Well, let me break it down for you, kid." Paulie dragged B.J. farther into the alley and sat him down on one of the fry shack's massive buckets of frying oil. "Listen up 'cause I'm only gonna explain this once. These B.L.A.S.T. guys—they're like a secret society of evil rockers, *comprende*? A really *old* secret society of evil rockers. And they work for the Overlord. They been watching you. B.L.A.S.T. has been watching you follow in the Good Supreme's footsteps, and now they think that *you* might be the next Supreme."

"Me?" A proud grin spread across B.J.'s face. "Seriously? They think that *I* could be the next—?"

"*Hey.*" Paulie whapped B.J. on the shoulder, nearly knocking him off his makeshift bucket-chair. "Keep your nose on, Ringo. This is not a good thing!"

"It's not?"

"No, it is not. It is a *bad, bad* thing." He pulled off his wraparound shades just to convey the gravity of the situation. "Try to understand this, kid. The Overlord is the reigning Megalord of Rock—the Gauntlet champion, the winner of just about everything."

"I know," B.J. said.

"Well, what do you think his greatest fear is? What do you think the *current* Megalord of Rock fears more than anything else in the world?"

B.J.'s eyes widened as the dawning revelation took shape. "The next Mega—?"

"You're damn *right*!" Paulie snapped. "He fears the next Megalord of Rock! He needs to hold on to his title. He can't let you usurp his throne, kid!"

"But come on." B.J. shrugged anxiously. "That's totally crazy. There's no way I could ever be the next Mega—"

"Of course it's crazy!" Paulie scoffed. "It is *stupidly* crazy. But you know who else is crazy? The *Overlord*. He's so triple loco, he's totally convinced that you're the next Supreme, and he's been sending out his B.L.A.S.T. minions so they can bring you back to him on a silver platter."

The awful combination of fear and fry grease was making B.J. doubly nauseated. "But I got away," he said. "I got away from the Overlord and I got away from B.L.A.S.T., so I'm safe, right?"

"Got away?" Paulie looked bowled over by B.J.'s apparent stupidity. "You're living with one of them right now!"

"What are you talking about?"

"The *dwarf*," Paulie growled. "The dwarf is B.L.A.S.T., fool! What have I been saying? They're supposed to bring you to the Overlord, and look where you are now. Who brought you here?

I'll give you a hint. He's three feet tall and he's got a head the size of a state fair melon!"

B.J. couldn't believe it. He wouldn't let himself believe it. There was no way Terry was B.L.A.S.T.

"No." B.J. shook his head repeatedly. "Terry's not B.L.A.S.T. You don't know what you're talking about."

"Don't you get it?" Paulie groaned. "That dwarf has you right where he wants you. He's dropping you right into the hands of the Overlord!"

"No, that's crazy," B.J. insisted. He stood up from his bucket and backed away from Paulie.

"Hey. Where do you think you're going? I need to get you out of here. We need to get out of this town pronto."

"Terry's not B.L.A.S.T." B.J. backed farther away. "You're making the whole thing up."

"It's the *truth*, kid. The dude is B.L.A.S.T., and he's got the horns to prove it."

"Horns? What horns? He doesn't have any horns."

"Not on his *head*, fool. The *tattoo.* He's got that devil horns tattoo just like all the other B.L.A.S.T. guys."

"He does not. I've never seen any tattoo."

"Don't you run again, kid. Now is not the time to run. Do you understand me?"

But that was exactly what B.J. did. He ran as fast as he possibly could. So fast that there was no way an old, wrinkled albino like Paulie could possibly catch him.

CHAPTER eleven

B.J.'s mother had always warned him that wearing black on the beach was a no-no. The blazing Jersey sun was cooking him like a hot dog spinning on a rotisserie of doom.

He'd been running for what felt like hours, even though it had only been minutes. He could feel the streams of perspiration running down his legs under his jeans. A nice cool pair of wrinkle-proof Dockers would have been a blessing right now, but his Docker days were long gone. He was Nigel "Hot Wings" Thunderdome now—the pretender to the throne of rock.

B.J. had been so caught up in his search for Sammy that he'd barely noticed where the Wünder-Bus had let him off in the first place. His only choice was to trust his sense of direction and hope for a glimpse of some middle schoolers and pirates, who would surely stand out from the crowd.

Miraculously, he found the bus parked near the site of the

old Asbury Park Carousel, which had been transformed from a terrifying cavalcade of petrified circus horses, spinning to the nightmarish sounds of a distorted pipe organ, into some kind of theater.

"Terry!" B.J. hollered with relief. "*Dude!*"

Terry was pacing back and forth behind the Wünder-Bus, puffing from his long, slim cigarette holder, his dark indigo scarf rippling in the wind. B.J. raced toward him as if he were a big purple finish line.

"Bloody hell!" Terry sighed with relief, wrapping his arms around B.J.'s waist and squeezing. "Where da heck have you *been*, mate? Dat wasn't no burger run, was it?"

"No," B.J. admitted. He doubled over and braced his knees, trying to catch his breath. "No, it wasn't a burger run. I was trying to find this girl."

"Well, tell me you found 'er at least because your band was starting to get a wee bit concerned, mate. We all was."

"I should go up and tell them I'm okay."

"Hold on there, mate." Terry pulled him back. "Don't worry about them. They're rehearsing for the big show tonight. Did you find your girl or not?"

"I did," B.J. panted. "I found her."

Terry grinned and jabbed B.J. in the gut. "Someone's got his self a groupie already. Nice one!"

"No, it's not like that," B.J. said. "It's way more complicated than that."

"Well, go on then," Terry said. "Give us the story. What's her name?"

"Her name is Sammy."

Terry's eyes lit up. "Sammy Springstein?"

"Yeah."

"*The* Sammy Springstein? Child prodigy? Offspring of the Overlord? Wickedest axe-chick under twenty-one in history?"

"Yeah, that one," B.J. said, trying to breathe in deep.

"You sly little foxy bastard!" Terry gave him two more excited jabs to the gut, and B.J. nearly lost his lunch. "Atta boy, mate! The young rock and roll prince finds himself a rock and roll princess! What did I *tell* you, son? This is Asbury Park! The Holy Land. Where dreams come true!"

"No, I'm *telling* you, Terry, it's not like that. She doesn't want to be my girlfriend. She wants me to play in a band with her."

"A band?" he marveled. This seemed to delight Terry even more than the thought of a royal rock and roll romance.

"A secret band," B.J. replied. "How insane is that?"

"Insane?" Terry looked almost offended by the term. "It ain't insane. It's bloody brilliant! The two of you together onstage—that's bloody magic, son! You'd tear this place apart! You'd take the Gauntlet for sure!"

B.J. couldn't believe his ears. "Terry, what are you talking about? What about the rules?"

"What rules?"

"The rules of the Gauntlet. You said we could only play in one band."

"Yeah, dat's right. So?"

"*So?* So what about the Good Supreme? What about my band?"

"What about 'em?"

"They're *my band*, that's what."

"Roight, mate, but we're talking about Sammy Springstein here. This is the chance of a loiftime."

"No, that's not why I'd do it," B.J. said. "It's just...If you'd heard her, Terry. I mean, if you'd seen her. She really needs me. She *needs* to win that money. It's, like, super important—life or death. I don't know what to do."

B.J. knocked his head back against the bus and stared up at the glaring sun, as if that would somehow give him answers. All it did was burn his eyes.

"Aw'ight, son, listen up. 'Cause I'm gonna tell it to you like it is. Let me ask you a question. You ever heard of a band called Little Boy Blue?"

"No."

"How about Raze? You ever heard of Raze?"

"No."

"Or the Strangeurs? Ever heard of 'em?"

"No, I've never heard of *any* bands."

"Well, it ain't just you," Terry said. "*No one's* ever heard of 'em. Little Boy Blue? Dat was Mick Jagger's band before he met Keith Richards. Raze? That was Jon Bon Jovi's first band when he was thirteen—just like you, mate. The Strangeurs was Steven Tyler's band way before Aerosmith."

"What's your point?"

"The point is, you *never* stay with your first band. The first band is just a stepping-stone. You've gotta take the next step, brother. You're gonna have to ditch these kids and start working with Sammy."

"Ditch them? I can't. I can't just ditch them. Can I?"

"I'll tell you what," Terry said. "If it'll make things easier for ya, I'll tell 'em myself. You just wait here, aw'ight?"

B.J. grabbed his shoulder. "No, wait. I don't think you should do this, Terry. I don't think you should tell them about this."

"He doesn't have to tell us," a startling voice chimed in from behind.

B.J. whipped around and found Jann standing right behind him, his arms tightly crossed over his chest and his eyes narrowed like a ruthless cowboy itching to draw his six-shooter. He was flanked by Layla and KeVonne. They looked nearly as angry as Jann. Sadness and disappointment were weighing down the corners of their mouths.

B.J. had no idea how long they'd been standing within earshot. Just long enough to get the worst possible impression.

"Yeah, I think we get the picture, Levine," Layla said. She tried to punish him with another angry stare, but she just ended up dropping her head and staring at the ground.

"No, wait a second, guys." B.J. could feel an imaginary cobra winding itself around his throat and cutting off his air supply. "Wait..."

"Wait for what, Beej?" Kev said. "Wait for you to officially dump us?"

"*No*, it's not like that. I wasn't going to dump—"

"No, you didn't even have the *guts* to dump us, Dockers." Jann said. "You were going to let *Terry* do it."

"No, I..."

"It's that girl, isn't it?" Layla looked so deflated—like someone had stuck a pin in her and let all the badass seep out. "That blond girl? You want to play with her instead of us, don't you?"

"*No*," B.J. groaned. He was still sweating like a roasted weenie, only now the hot sun had nothing to do with it.

"Don't lie, Levine," Layla said. "You're a terrible liar."

"No, I'm—I mean, *yes*, it's that girl, but I didn't say I would play with her yet."

"*Yet?*" Kev squawked. "Oh, so you were just gonna wait a little longer before you told us?"

"No, that's not what I meant!"

Jann threw up his arms. "Dudes, I've heard enough. You know what? I'm gonna bounce. I didn't come all the way out here for this. You guys coming?"

"I'm right behind you, man," Kev said.

"Yeah, me too." Layla turned away and followed Jann and Kev down the road.

B.J. started to race after them. "Guys, come on! Please wait!"

Jann spun around and thrust his palm in B.J.'s face. "*Don't* try to follow us, Dockers. It's a real waste of time. We followed you all the way out here and look where it got us."

"No, but, Jann..."

"Don't worry about us," Jann said. "We'll find our own ride home."

The three of them turned back around in unison and picked up their speed, heading farther down the street.

B.J. tried to follow them again, but this time Terry held him back.

"Let 'em go, mate," he said quietly. "It's for the best. Believe me."

B.J.'s stomach twisted into tight, inhuman knots as he stared at the backs of his three closest friends: a black leather jacket, a red rumpled jumpsuit, and a canary yellow T-shirt—all disappearing into the huge rocker crowd.

His eyes settled on Layla's jet-black hair, bobbing up and down as she sulked her way down the road. He stared at the back of her head, praying for her to turn around and give him one more chance to explain.

And she did. She did turn back to him. But only for a split second. And then she turned away for good.

"Don't worry, mate," Terry said. "Someone will drive them back for sure. Come on, let's go find little Ms. Springstein so you can get to work on that secret band." He tried to wrap his arm around B.J.'s waist, but B.J. pulled away.

"Get off me," B.J. snapped. "I think you've helped enough, Terry. I'll find her myself."

And then, despite his heavy heart, and even heavier, throbbing legs, he was running again. Running back to search for the one friend he had left.

★ ★ ★

"Sammy?"

He called out as loudly as he could while still maintaining a whisper. He was terrified of another run-in with the Overlord, but this was where he'd promised to meet her—next to the smelly tie-dyed dumpster behind a row of three tour buses.

"Sammy? Are you here? Sammy? I came back like I promised." He peered around the back of the dumpster. "Where are you?"

There was no response. Just the sound of another lousy band, jamming on their pig-nose amps next to a beat-up puke-green

Chevy van. The band had painted their name in frilly red calligraphy on the side of the van, but the logo didn't fit the band name at all: *Burrito Butt.*

Burrito Butt's guitar player was scribbling on his notepad as he shrieked out a song that was clearly a work in progress.

NIGHT! Surrender! The darkness of the night.
The CHAINS of DOOM will chain you
To the chains of the niiiight...

"*No.* No, that totally sucks." Burrito Butt stopped himself mid-song, just exactly as B.J.'s father had done a million times before. "Okay, let's try it from the top." He began to shriek again. "*NIGHT! Surrender. The darkness of the niiiight. A CHAIN of rocks will DOOM you...*No. *A rock of stones will chain you...*"

The horrid sounds of Burrito Butt were pushing B.J. to the edge. He had somehow managed to lose his band in a matter of minutes and now it was beginning to look like he'd lost Sammy too. Her turquoise camping chair was gone. He gave up on his timid half-whispers and called over to Burrito Butt.

"Excuse me! Burrito Butt! Do you guys know Sammy Springstein?"

The lead singer cut off his song and turned back to B.J. His nose looked like it had been broken at least twice, and he had a long lime-green ponytail, along with a lip ring in each corner of his mouth. "Um, *duh*," he said in an oddly high-pitched voice. "The Overlord's little princess? Of course we know Sammy."

"Well, did you see her here? She was playing guitar right over here in a little fold-out chair."

"Nah, we just pulled in a few minutes ago. We would have noticed her, dude. We definitely would have noticed the Overlord's tour bus."

"Yeah, it's pretty hard to miss the Over-bus," the bass player laughed. "Hey, wait…Aren't you the British kid from the Fire Pit? Dude, you totally *rocked* last night. You're him, right?"

"Yeah," B.J. mumbled. "I'm the British kid."

That's when it really hit him.

She didn't even know his name. How could she come looking for him if she didn't know his name? She didn't really know anything about him because everything he'd told her was a lie.

He leaned back against the dumpster and slid to the ground with a thud. How could B.L.A.S.T. have even thought for a moment that B.J. Levine was the next Megalord of Rock? Would a true Megalord of Rock abandon his own band—even if he hadn't exactly done it on purpose? Would a true Megalord of Rock steal his father's songs because he couldn't write any of his own? Would a true Megalord convince a desperate girl that he was someone that he wasn't?

No. A true Megalord would stick with his band until the end. He would write his own songs. He would speak the Truth with a capital T. And now, thanks to Sammy Springstein, B.J. had officially decided. He was not going to be a fake half-lord anymore. He was going to be real.

He had to tell her the whole story from the very beginning. He had to tell her absolutely everything because only then would she understand why he had to do what he had to do.

But how was he going to tell her? She didn't have a cell phone or an email address. There was only one thing he could think of. One way that might work. He was going to have to kick it old school.

"Hey, Burrito Butt!" he called out, as he picked himself up and dusted himself off.

"Yeah, wassup British kid who doesn't sound British?"

"Could I borrow some paper and a pen?" B.J. asked. "I need to write someone a letter."

"Nice," Burrito Butt smiled. "Kicking it old school. Very romantic."

"It's not *like* that," B.J. groaned as he took a notepad and a pen from Burrito Butt.

Dear Sammy,

Hi, it's me, Nigel. I mean, not Nigel, but I'll explain that in a second.

Sammy, I'm writing to find out if you are okay. Are you okay? And also, where are you? You took off so fast, I didn't get a chance to say goodbye to you, so I have to write you this letter because I'm not supposed to talk to you, and you don't have an email address, and there are some way important things I need to tell you...

He scribbled away on the notepad, churning out page after page, telling Sammy all about his real name and his boring origins in Cleveland and his general Jewishness and his father's weirdly beloved quilt. He tried his best to describe everything that had happened to him since the moment he first met Merv at his apartment—all the way up to this very moment, sitting against a tie-dye dumpster in a Jersey Shore parking lot, listening to the not-so-sweet sounds of Burrito Butt, writing to a girl he hardly knew but somehow felt totally connected to.

The thing is, Sammy, I could probably go on for a lot longer, but I kind of have to hurry it up if I'm going to try to find my band and get us back together.

I guess that's what I'm trying to tell you with my whole story. Now that you've read all about Kev and Layla and Jann, I'm hoping you'll understand why I have to play the Gauntlet with them if they'll still let me. If there's any way on the planet that we can win it, then I could give you my part of the money and you could try to find your mom. But I can't start a secret band with you tonight, Sammy. I'm really, really sorry, but I can't. I'm just trying to speak the Truth with a capital T because that's what a true Megalord would do.

The truth is, Kev and Layla and Jann are the only reason I'm here. Kev started a band with me when I couldn't even sing. Layla believed in me when my only song was "911 Emergency Toast." Jann killed Lola for me, Sammy. I almost got them all killed by biker hobos, and they're still here. They've stuck with me through everything. And I can't let them down now.

I only hope that this letter makes it to you. And I really hope you'll try to find me at the Gauntlet, wherever you are. Otherwise, I'm going to have to find you. And one way or another, I will find you. I'll keep listening for your song.

Your friend (hopefully forever),
Benjamin James Levine

B.J. folded the letter in quarters, wrote Sammy's name on the top, and handed it to Burrito Butt. The lead singer promised that if Sammy returned to that spot that he would give her the letter. It was all B.J. could think to do.

With the letter safely in Burrito Butt's hands, B.J. turned around and began his new quest: to find his band and get them back together in time for the Gauntlet tonight.

Unfortunately, he was only about thirty yards into his new quest when Terry the Wünder-Dwarf scurried up from behind and blocked his path.

★ ★ ★

"Good God, mate! I been searchin' for you everywhere!"

Terry was soaked with sweat and severely out of breath. He took in great big gulps of air and leaned against B.J. as if he were a lamppost. "Why'd you have to run off like that? Are you completely daft?"

"I'm sorry, Terry, but I can't talk now," B.J. explained. "I have to try and find my band."

"*What?* Your band's long gone, man. They must have found a ride by now." Terry searched the edges of the parking lot. "Where's Sammy? Ain't you two writing up a brilliant song for tonoight?"

"I'm not sure where she is, but right now I've got to look for Layla and the guys. Maybe they haven't found a ride yet and I can still fix this." He tried to step around Terry, but Terry kept his stubby fingers glued to his T-shirt.

"*Hold on*, mate. Are you forgettin' everything I told you? You can't miss this chance. We gotta find Sammy and get you two together to make history!"

B.J. tried to politely remove Terry's hand from his shirt. "Terry, you've been awesome to me and you've totally made me feel like I can do this, but I've got to do it with the Good Supreme, not with Sammy, okay?" He went to work on Terry's individual fingers, but now Terry was clinging to him with both hands like a giant needy parrot.

"I can't let you do that, mate. You've got to play with Sammy tonight or you'll be makin' the biggest mistake of your life."

"Come on, Terry. Let *go*."

"Ain't happenin'."

B.J. was dragging Terry along with each slow and labored step, digging his fingertips into Terry's kung-fu grip, trying to pry himself loose. "Terry, I need to go!"

"Over my dead body, mate! You're throwing your life away and you don't even know it!"

Now it was a full-on wrestling match. Scrawny Early-Growth-Spurt Boy vs. Soaking Wet Pirate Dwarf with Parrot Claws. They were spinning each other in circles—grunting, straining, pushing, tugging.

B.J. gave up on the fingers and went to work on Terry's arms. He started clawing at anything he could: Terry's long brown hair; the frills of his pirate shirt; the elastic of his spandex pants; and then, finally, his trademark, flowing indigo scarf. He tugged so hard that he actually managed to pull the scarf clean off. And that's when he saw it.

"AAAAAAAAHHHHHH!"

"What?" Terry jumped away, his face frozen with shock and his cheeks beet-red from the tussle. "Did I hurt ya, mate? I didn't mean to hurt ya!"

"Horns," B.J. murmured, stepping backward.

"What? What are you on about?"

"Devil horns." B.J.'s finger rose up and pointed to the tattoo on the side of Terry's neck—the neck that had always been covered by a flowing purple scarf.

It was the symbol. The sign of the devil horns.

"Oh my God, Paulie was telling the *truth*." B.J. started backing away. "You're one of *them*. You're *B.L.A.S.T.*"

Terry brought his hand to his neck, finally realizing that his scarf was now in B.J.'s tightly clenched fist. The look in Terry's eyes shifted to something very cautious and deliberate. He raised his arms out slowly, as if B.J. was wielding a weapon. "Aw'ight, mate, just stay calm. This ain't what you think, aw'ight. Just stay cool."

"I trusted you," B.J. breathed. "I can't believe I trusted you." He dropped the scarf to the ground and took off through the parking lot, but Terry raced after him.

"Ah, jeez. Don't run!" Terry moaned. "I'm exhawsted, kid! I can't keep up with yous anymore. Can ya' *please* stop the runnin'?"

B.J. stopped in his tracks and turned around, staring dumbfounded at Terry. Something about him was suddenly very different. "Your accent...What happened to your English accent?"

"Forget about it!" Terry bellowed. Suddenly, his accent sounded just like Merv's and Paulie's and everyone else B.J. had ever met from the state of New Jersey. "They thought you'd trust a guy with an English accent more. What can I say? I *told* them it was dumb."

"Oh my God, you're not even *British*?"

"Look, just *don't run*," Terry begged. "Please, just give me a chance to explain, kid. We ain't got time for any more of these game. You only got a few more hours. You gotta play with Sammy tonight and that's awl there is to it. This is our last chance. Just come with me and we can find her together." Terry reached out, but B.J. snapped his arm away.

"I'm not going anywhere with you! You're trying to bring me to the Overlord so he can kill me!"

"*What?*" Terry shook his head. "No, no, no, no. You don't know what ya' tawking about. B.L.A.S.T. ain't trying to *kill* you, brother. We're the *good guys.*"

"The good guys? Oh, is that why you made up a fake English accent and kidnapped me and brought me to the Jersey Shore?"

"We didn't kidnap you. We just helped you get where you needed to be."

"You tried to throw me in a van! Isn't that, like, the *definition* of kidnapping?"

"We didn't have a choice! You tried to run away at the station, and we had to get you to Sammy by any means necessary. She's your *Sacred Pinky*, man."

B.J. cocked his head to the side. "Sammy? What does Sammy have to do with it?"

"Sammy has *everything* to do with it!" Terry closed his eyes and tried to go to a calmer place. He slowly reopened his eyes and spoke in more measured tones. "Kid, just listen. It's time you found out what's really going on here."

"Oh, *now* it's time?"

"I said listen!"

B.J. zipped his lip.

"B.L.A.S.T.," Terry said. "Do you even know what it stands for?"

"No."

"It's the Bayonne League of Angels for the Sacred Two."

"The Sacred Two? What is that?"

Terry reached for B.J.'s hand. B.J. pulled away with a start, but Terry calmly took hold of his fingers.

"Relax. I just want to show you." Terry molded B.J.'s hand into the devil horns position—extending his index finger and pinky and wrapping his thumb around his other two fingers.

"Ya see, kid, every great rock band in history has got a Sacred Two—a Sacred Finger and a Sacred Pinky. That's where this hand sign came from." He wiggled B.J.'s index finger. "The index finger represents the front man. He's the number one—the charismatic leader with the golden pipes and the inspiration for all the songs. And the pinky," he wiggled B.J.'s pinky, "that's the wing man—the number two. The one who inspires the front man. The one who believes in him no matter what. Who helps him bring all his songs to life. Together, they form the Sacred Two. I'm tawking about all the great Sacred Twos: Mick and Keith, Plant and Page, Axl and Slash, Tyler and Perry, White and White, Bon Jovi and Sambora. B.L.A.S.T. helped bring all those epic pairings together, even though they never knew it."

"What do you mean 'helped' bring them together?"

"We see the potential in a Sacred Two, and we make sure they come together, that's all. We make sure they're in the right place at the right time so they can discover each other and start their rocking journey to greatness."

"You're saying that B.L.A.S.T. is the reason Mick Jagger and Keith Richards got together?"

"No, I'm just saying we *helped*. It was all about getting those two kids to meet at the same train station in 1960. We had to get this stack of R&B records into Mick's hand. It was real complicated."

"But that was, like, a *million* years ago."

"We been around *forever*, kid. Why do you think we're all so damn old? We been bringing 'em together since the late fifties. There's a British League, a Boston League, a Bayshore League.

We all help each other out, but me and Merv, we're with the Bayonne League. And we just happen to know that you and Sammy Springstein are Bayonne's next Sacred Two. You two are gonna be the second coming of Jovi, dude. You're gonna change New Jersey rock as we know it!"

B.J. searched Terry's eyes to see if he could possibly be serious. "Okay, that's the craziest thing I've ever heard."

"Yeah, crazy 'cause it's *true*," Terry growled. "We been working on this one for years, but we could never find a way to bring you two kids together. 'Hot Wings' and your mom had you hiding out in the middle of Iowa or something and the Overlord keeps Sammy on the road, moving around so fast that we can never keep up. But, see, we *knew* he'd have to come back to the Gauntlet to defend his title and we knew he'd bring Sammy with him. And when we finally found you in New York, we knew it was destiny. That's what Merv was trying to tell your folks. He wanted them to bring you to the Gauntlet so you and Sammy could finally get together. But your folks weren't having it, so we had to get you here on your own. That's why we left you the book."

"What do you mean 'left me' the book? I found the book."

"Nah, you didn't find nothin', kid. We made that book up for *you*. Merv left it where he knew you'd see it. That was our Plan B if your folks wouldn't take you on the road. It was the only way. We had put you through every trial in that book so we could mold you into the front man you were born to be. You had to be a Sacred Finger worthy of Sammy's Sacred Pinky before we could lead you to the Holy Land."

"But how did you even know I'd do it? How did you know I'd do anything the book said?"

"Because you're a born rocker, kid, and all rockers are rebels. We knew once you read Merv's warning you'd do whatever he told you *not* to do. It's in your blood, bro. Don't you get it yet? That's how we knew you and Sammy were the next Sacred Two. We've known since you were tiny babies. You're both the children of Bayonette—the greatest Jersey rock band the world never knew. Bayonette was on their way to becoming the next Megalords until your psycho dad had to go and break up the band in '99."

"Wait. Hot Wings broke up the band?"

"No, your *dad* broke up the band."

"But Hot Wings *is* my dad."

"Oh…" Terry's eyes drifted down to B.J.'s feet. "Uh…" His head began to veer in every direction but B.J.'s. "Yeah, okay…I should have thought that one through better. This ain't the way to tell you about that."

B.J. felt a cold chill in his belly. He felt that numbness in his fingers and his tongue and that disorienting dizziness in his head. "Tell me what?" He heard himself asking the question, but his mind was way ahead of him—putting pieces together that had been rolling around in the back of his head for years.

He was thinking about all those years of unbearable distance with his father. Maybe Jayson Levine had never acted like B.J.'s dad because he *wasn't* B.J.'s dad.

"Yeah...Hot Wings ain't your dad, kid," Terry said plainly. "Your real pop is Damian 'The Overlord' Springstein."

B.J.'s legs felt incredibly wobbly—like they were about to give out. "The Overlord is my dad," B.J. said between shallow breaths. "My dad is the Overlord." All he could do was repeat the words, standing in a near-catatonic state. "The Overlord is my dad. My dad is the...*Wait.* Are you telling me that Sammy is my *sister*?"

"Hey, slow down there, Skywalker. I didn't say that either."

"But then how...?"

"See, you don't know nothin', kid. You don't know nothin' about your life or your past. You don't even know your real name."

"I do too! It's Benjamin James Levine."

"*Benjamin James?* You really think the Overlord would name his kid somethin' as plain as 'Benjamin James'? The guy who changed his own name to Springstein?"

"Then what's my name?"

"B.J.?" Terry stared at him. "You can't be that thick, kid. *B.J.* What do you *think* your name is? Your name is *Bon Jovi*, dude!

Of *course* it's Bon Jovi. *Bon* as in the Latin root meaning 'good.' *Jovi*, as in 'of Jove' or 'God-like,' 'the supreme.' Am I getting *through* to you, kid? You *are* the Good Supreme. You always *have* been the Good Supreme, and you and Sammy were *born* to play together. It's a *prophecy*, dude!"

B.J.'s head was about to spin its way right off his neck. It was too much information—too much completely insane information pouring in at once.

B.J. stared down at Terry's head for at least three full seconds. "Okay, are *all* New Jersey rockers total lunatics?"

"We ain't lunatics," Terry said. "We're just keeping the faith, man. I know you've only been in Jersey for like a day, but you're gonna need to understand something. Here in Jersey, it ain't just rock and roll. It's a religion."

"Terry," B.J. said. "I'm just a scrawny Jew from New York, but I think you need to understand something too. You B.L.A.S.T. guys...are *total psychos.*"

B.J. launched himself into a full-scale gallop, sprinting from Terry as fast as he possibly could.

"No. Don't run again!" Terry hollered. "NO GO, NO GO! HE'S RUNNIN', BOYS! WE GOT A RUNNER!"

A chorus of kick-starting engines erupted from behind, roaring through the parking lot like instant thunder. B.J. glimpsed over his shoulder just long enough to see the sprawling armada of gleaming

Harleys and red bandannas spewing out from behind the tour buses like jet-powered robo-roaches—headed up by none other than Merv himself.

B.J. would have screamed if he wasn't committing every last ounce of his energy to his throbbing legs. He was no match for their 80-horsepower Harleys. It was only a matter of time before he ran out of buses parked so close together that a hulking bike couldn't follow him. Maybe he was destined to be just one thing: roadkill.

"Hold on, Scarecrow! I'm comin'!"

B.J. froze at the edge of the parking lot, gluing himself to the side of the last bus, watching B.L.A.S.T.'s Harleys circle around like a herd of velociraptors. A monstrous, black, double-decker tour bus barreled across the road at breakneck speed, its door swinging wide open. It cut right through the circle of Harleys like a giant T-Rex, butting away the helpless raptors with its gargantuan head. The monster bus spun out to a full stop, its piercing breaks even sounding like the screech of an angry T-Rex announcing its total dominance.

Albino Paulie had one hand on the steering wheel and one hand on the bus door lever. B.J. had never been so happy to see a pale-eyed, tissue-paper freak in his entire life.

"Get in!" Paulie shouted.

B.J. wasted no time. He leapt over the parking lot rails and climbed the bus's steps in one stride. Paulie stepped on the gas, kicking the rolling T-Rex into overdrive.

B.J. smushed his face to the window just in time to catch a last glimpse of Merv and his B.L.A.S.T. crew trying to walk their battered bikes back onto the road. There was no way they'd be able to catch up now.

"Ugh, thank God," B.J. sighed, taking his first real breath in minutes as he fell back against the steps. "*Thank you*, Paulie. Thank you, thank you, thank you. I should have trusted you the whole time."

"No worries, Scarecrow," Paulie said, swerving his way down Ocean Avenue. "Just step on board and try to chill. I got someone here who wants to talk to you."

"Who?" B.J. gathered himself and climbed the rest of the way onto the bus. He nearly fell back again when he saw them.

Layla, Kev, and Jann were sitting in the dark bus's kitchen area, sipping on cans of Red Bull.

B.J.'s eyes lit up with joy. "What are you guys doing here?"

But his joyful expression was not returned. They were all still angry at him. They would barely look him in the eye. Layla was the only one who'd even speak.

"Paulie found us looking for a ride," she mumbled. "He said he'd drive us back to the city."

"Oh. Cool," B.J. said meekly. He couldn't stand the way Layla was talking to him. Like he'd let her down in every possible way. Like she hardly even knew him.

He hadn't prepared his apology and rallying speech for the band yet. He was going to have to improvise, and that was a skill he clearly did not possess. He opened his mouth to give it his best shot, but then, for the first time since he'd leaped aboard, he noticed the bus's décor.

Every inch of the bus was goth. The carpet looked like black velvet and so did the curtains, which were hanging from heavy steel chains. The seats were black patent leather with gaudy, jeweled armrests. And sitting in little glass cabinets were a seemingly endless supply of jewel-encrusted goblets, lined up one after the other like trophies.

This could only be one man's tour bus.

A narrow door creaked open from the back, and that very man stepped out onto the black velvet carpet—so tall that his jagged, teased-out Medusa hair nearly hit the ceiling; so slim that his full-length, leather trench coat made him look like a Ringwraith with purple-blue eyes buried under mounds of black eyeliner and mascara.

How could B.J. not have noticed it before? It was like looking at a picture of himself from the future—some strange alternate future where he had really embraced leather and eye makeup.

"Hello, B.J.," the Overlord said.

They faced each other from either end of the bus like some kind of high noon, rocker showdown.

"You know my real name," B.J. said, surprised.

"Of course I know your name," the Overlord said. "I'm the one who gave it to you."

B.J. tried to hide the slight tremors in his legs. He turned back to Paulie as his eyes grew tense with worry. "You…You're with him. You've been with him the whole time."

"Just tawk to him," Paulie said, keeping his eyes on the road. "Listen to what he has to say."

"Um, excuse me," Kev raised his hand. "I'm a little lost here. Can someone tell me what the heck is—" Layla elbowed him in the ribs to shut him up.

The Overlord stepped to the side of the doorway and beckoned B.J. in. "Come on, son. Let's talk. It's been way too long."

B.J. looked behind him and then back to the Overlord.

"I said let's talk!" the Overlord barked.

There was simply nowhere left to run. B.J. bowed his head and began his slow death march down the black velvet carpet.

CHAPTER twelve

The Overlord pulled B.J. into a small room at the back of the bus and slammed the door behind him. "Okay, son, where's Sammy?"

"Don't call me that," B.J. said, trying to mask his fear.

"Why can't I call you 'son'? It's the truth, you know."

"No, it's not." B.J. was, of course, lying. He'd somehow known it was the truth from the moment Terry let the cat out of the bag.

"Let's not fight, son." The Overlord flashed all his teeth in a pathetic attempt at a smile. He took a step forward, and B.J. flinched, backing into the corner of the cramped little room. He felt like he was trapped in a tiny cage with a very tall black bear.

When he glanced around the room, he realized that it *was* a cage of sorts. It was Sammy's cage. There was a row of vintage guitars propped up on stands, and a cheesy, fake marble table littered with her notebooks and guitar picks. Sammy's little sleeper bed was in the corner, next to her open closet, which was filled with bright orange clothes. Her "bedroom window" was actually the bus's rear window, and B.J. was struck with a vivid image of Sammy, staring out at the sun like a prisoner, strumming her guitar as she watched miles of road disappear into the horizon.

"Just tell me where she is," the Overlord said, "and we'll get along fine."

"I don't know where she is," B.J. said. "I thought she was with you."

"Don't lie to me, son! The Gauntlet is going down in a few hours and I am short one guitar player!"

"I'm not lying! I don't know where she is, and *stop* calling me that!"

"Okay, okay. Let's just take it down a notch." The Overlord flashed another forced, toothy grin. "What say we sit down and have ourselves a little man-to-man? It's long overdue, don't you think?"

B.J. couldn't believe it. He'd been waiting for his father to call him a man since he was eleven years old. It was just the wrong father.

"Okay," he said cautiously. It wasn't as if he had many choices.

They each pulled a chair up to the marble table and sat down face-to-face. Damian leaned forward on his elbows, invading B.J.'s personal space with his lengthy torso. B.J. leaned back as far as he could without tipping over.

"I got to tell you, son..." Damian shook his head with amazement. "You were really something at the Fire Pit last night. I always knew you'd be something special, man. You made me proud."

B.J. was struck silent. There were only two things he'd wanted to hear from his father his whole life, and the Overlord had just said both of them in less than a minute.

"Thanks," he croaked.

"Well, I'm just speaking the truth," Damian said. "That's what us Megalords do, right?"

"I'm trying to," B.J. said. He couldn't help being flattered when Damian referred to him as a fellow Megalord.

"You know," Damian said. "I just want to say...I'm really sorry I haven't been there for you, son. There ain't no excuse for it except selfishness."

This was not the conversation B.J. had expected. "Um...that's okay?" he mumbled. What else what he was supposed to say?

"The truth is..." Damian bowed his head. "I've always kind of wanted a son. I never should have left you in the first place."

"Then why did you? I don't understand what happened."

"Oh, that is a *long* story," Damian laughed bitterly. "I'm just saying it would have been pretty cool, you know? You and me on the road, playing music. Don't get me wrong, I love Sammy to death, but what do I really know about raising a teenage girl? I just buy her as many orange clothes as I can find, you know?"

"Yeah, what's with all the orange?" B.J. looked back at Sammy's closet.

"I got no idea," Damian replied. "It's always been her thing. Something about it reminding of her of her favorite baby blanket or something. Look, son, the point is, I want to apologize. I never should have yelled at you like I did. That's just how a dad gets when he sees a musician talking to his daughter. I didn't even know who you were until today. The important thing is that I know now and I'm hoping we can still make it right. Can't you picture it? You, me, and Sammy on the road together as a family? I've seen what you can do, kid. We could totally rule the rock scene as father and son. It could be so beautiful. What do you think? Can we make peace?"

"I don't know," B.J. said. It was an awfully intriguing picture. B.J. and Sammy on the road together. A family of rockers touring the world. It was the total opposite of B.J.'s painfully boring life.

Damian bent down and opened a cabinet next to Sammy's mini-fridge. He pulled out two of his trademark jeweled goblets and handed one to B.J. "Just have a drink with me, son."

"A *drink* drink?"

"Just juice," Damian laughed, as he pulled a little bottle of pomegranate juice from the inside pocket of his leather coat. "I live on this stuff. You know, for the antioxidants." He poured some of the red, syrupy juice into his own goblet and then into B.J.'s. "When rockers make peace, we don't shake on it. We drink on it." He raised his goblet to B.J. "What do you say, son? Will you drink with me?"

B.J. looked at his goblet and slowly raised it up. "I, uh…I don't know what to say."

"I know you're confused," Damian said. "You don't have to say anything right now. Just share this one drink with me. It would mean a lot to me. Come on, son. Truce?"

B.J. peered at the viscous liquid in the goblet. Pomegranate juice was seriously disgusting. But if one drink could keep the Overlord smiling, this didn't seem like the best time to rock the boat. He clinked goblets with his father.

"Truce," he agreed. He brought the cup to his lips and tipped it back.

"Bacon!" KeVonne burst through the doorway, his eyes ablaze with hunger. "Do I smell *bacon* in here? Are you eating bacon without me, Beej?"

Bacon? Why is Kev smelling bacon?

B.J.'s eyes darted back to the goblet as the blood-red juice rolled toward his lips. It all came back to him in a flash. Terry's tragic story. The tale of Vince Moretti: a skinny rocker with a big, bright future until that one fateful night in New Jersey when someone slipped him a nasty concoction with pork-like odor…

"Hemrock!" B.J. screamed, hurling the goblet to the floor just before the poison had touched his lips. "You're trying to give me hemrock!"

"Beat it, Bootsy!" The Overlord shoved KeVonne out of the room with one hand, slammed the door closed, and locked it. He whirled back around to B.J., goblet in hand, and all that fake kindness had drained away from his cold purple eyes. "You're going to drink this, kid. We're not leaving this room until you do." He lunged forward, and B.J. leaped back onto Sammy's bed, crashing into the corner.

"Stay away from me!" he hollered. But the Overlord hurled the table aside and lunged again—this time managing to grab B.J.'s wrist with his long, bony fingers. He tugged him closer, gripping the back of his neck, trying to force his head down toward the goblet.

"Just drink the pork juice, son! It ain't gonna hurt ya! Come on, open up for the choo-choo. *Toot-toot…*"

"No!" B.J. grabbed the Overlord's forearm with both hands, struggling to pull the goblet away from his mouth. "You're trying to turn me into another Rodeo Pig! That was *you*, wasn't it? You're the one who poisoned Vince Moretti!"

"I don't know what you're talking about. Just *drink*."

"Let *go* of me!"

B.J. could hear his bandmates pounding at the door. "What's going on in there?" Jann called out.

"Are you okay, Levine?" Layla shouted.

"He's fine!" The Overlord called back. "He just needs to take his medicine!" He had nearly tipped the goblet into B.J.'s mouth when B.J. slithered free from his grip and jumped into Sammy's closet. He tried to shut the sliding door, but the Overlord got his hand on the outside handle and they were stuck in a deadlock—B.J. straining with both hands to shut the door; his father using his one free hand to keep it open.

"Why are you *doing* this?" B.J. hollered. His face and neck were burning with effort.

"There can be only *one*."

"One what?"

"One Megalord! One Supreme! I ain't about to let you steal my Sacred Pinky!"

"Oh, *please* tell me you're not serious."

"You think this is a joke? I ain't just doing this for me, son. I'm doing this for the entire state of New Jersey!"

"What is the *matter* with you Jersey rockers? Are you *all* completely nuts? How do you even know I'm the next Supreme? You've only heard me sing once!"

"I've known it since you were a *baby.* That's when Merv told us the prophecy."

"Oh, like hearing it from one goat-faced biker freak makes it true?"

"That goat-faced biker freak was responsible for the Rolling Stones, Aerosmith, and Led Zeppelin! And he wasn't always so goat-faced."

"Hel-*lo!* He's making it all up, dude! They're just a bunch of demented old guys from Bayonne!"

"He ain't making nothin' up, son! I knew it was true from the first time I heard you cry."

"What?"

"Every time you cried, you'd scream out a perfect G-sharp. When you were hungry, it was a perfect A above middle C. You tell me what kind of six-month-old baby has *perfect pitch*? You could see it in everyone's faces—at the grocery store, at McDonald's—the way one of your little baby screams would stop them all in their tracks and command their attention; the way their faces would freeze up and they'd just stare at you, transfixed. That's how I knew it was true. That's how I knew you were the Supreme. 'Cause you've been doing it since you were born."

"Doing what? Screaming?"

"You're not just screaming! You're *rocking their faces,* son."

"What?"

"Oh, come *on*! Don't tell me you ain't noticed it every time you scream. Don't tell me you ain't noticed the look in people's eyes? You're rocking every one of those faces and there ain't no one else on this Earth with the mystical power to rock faces besides the original Good Supreme himself, Mr. Jon Bon Jovi! And believe me, I have tried!"

The entire room suddenly swerved to the left. B.J. thought it was a massive attack of vertigo until the Overlord went flying across the room and the sound of screeching brakes erupted beneath their feet. B.J. was launched from the floor, tumbling up against his father like a crash test dummy. The goblet flew from the Overlord's hands, splattering the hemrock all over the floor, where it frothed and bubbled on the carpet. The long, deafening screech of the brakes finally came to an end, and everything went deathly still.

What just happened? Did we just crash? B.J. checked for feeling in his arms and legs—everything appeared to be working properly. He heard a pounding coming from the front of the bus, like someone was knocking violently on the bus's front door.

"Uh, Damian!" Paulie called from up front. "Damian, we got a major problem up here. I think you wanna get out here, man."

B.J. and the Overlord carefully untangled their arms and legs, climbed slowly to their feet, and dusted themselves off. The Overlord jumped ahead, unlocked the bedroom door, and swung it open. When B.J. peered over his shoulder, he thought he was having some sort of hallucination induced by severe head trauma.

He saw the two of them standing together at the front of the bus, arms crossed over their chests like superheroes, eviscerating the Overlord with their angry stares. But they weren't hallucinations; they were real. Jayson and Diana Levine were real.

"Mom…? Dad…?"

B.J.'s parents opened their arms, as his mother's eyes grew moist with tears. He elbowed the Overlord out of the way and ran down the aisle, barreling into them and squeezing until he could feel their ribs.

"How?" His head was nestled between their faces. "How did you find me?"

"We were already here," Dad said, pulling him closer. "Once we put the pieces together, I knew those B.L.A.S.T. psychos had found some way to bring you to the Gauntlet." He tightened his grip around B.J., squeezing him like he'd been missing for months. "I thought I'd lost you too."

"What do you mean lost me too?"

"We've been looking for you all day," Mom said. "We just got a call from Merv that you were headed up Ocean Avenue in Damian's bus."

"We had to cut you off at the pass," Dad said.

B.J. looked through the windshield and saw their Dodge Durango parked at an odd angle in the middle of Ocean Avenue. They'd left Paulie no choice but to throw on the brakes and swerve to a halt.

"Why don't you take a seat, son?" Dad guided B.J. to a seat next to Layla, ran his hand through his scruffy hair, and then he did something he probably hadn't done in five years. He kissed B.J. on the cheek. "You're okay, dude? Nothing bruised or broken?"

B.J. felt like he'd aged about ten years since the last time he'd seen his dad, but right now, he couldn't help smiling like a little kid. "I'm okay, Dad. Really."

"Good," Dad said. "Because if anyone ever tried to hurt you, Beej, then it would be *real* hard for me not to take him by his big goblin ears and crush his ugly goblin face into tiny little chunks of *chopped meat.*" He ripped off his shades and threw them down on an empty seat. "You," he murmured, pointing his long finger at the Overlord like a dagger. "Get out."

The Overlord laughed. "What are you talking about, Jay? This is *my* bus."

"OUT!" Jayson bellowed. It was the loudest B.J. had ever heard his dad scream without singing. "I don't want you within a hundred feet of my son."

"He ain't your son, Jay. He's my son."

"No, *you* don't get to call him that." Jayson leaped at Damian and snatched the lapels of his leather coat. "He is *my* son, Damian. I've raised him since he was a baby, and I've loved him since he was a baby, and he probably doesn't even know that. He probably thinks I'm some kind of cold, distant jerk, and he doesn't even know why. He doesn't know how *scared* I am to get close to him because I'm so scared I'm going to lose him! I'm so scared that *you're* going to sneak into my house and steal him away from me. That was the plan, right? You were going to try to steal my son away from me—just like you stole Sammy?"

"Not exactly," Damian replied.

"Well, *what* then? What was the plan, Dame?"

"Hemrock," B.J. said. "He tried to give me—"

"*Hemrock?*" Jayson's pale cheeks turned pink with rage. "You tried to give my boy *hemrock*? Is that even a *real thing*?"

The bus went momentarily silent. It hadn't even occurred to B.J. that hemrock might not be a real thing—that Vince Moretti might have just eaten an enormous amount of Finnish bacon, gotten enormously fat, and lost his voice over the years. After all, Terry was the one who'd told them the tale of the Rodeo Pig, and those B.L.A.S.T. folks' sanity was questionable at best.

"Shame on you, Damian!" Mom elbowed Jayson out of the way so she could get up in the Overlord's face. "Shame on you for scaring a defenseless thirteen-year-old boy!" She punched him hard in the shoulder. "Shame on you for what you and those B.L.A.S.T. nuts have done to our families. Shame on you for still believing in this stupid prophecy! We had to move to Cleveland just to keep you people away from him!"

"It is not nonsense," Damian insisted. "I didn't want to scare him, but the kid's my competition. You know the rules, Diana. There can be only *one*."

She socked him in the arm again. "That's it!"

Mom grabbed hold of his arm and dragged him up the aisle toward the bus's front door.

"Hey! You can't throw me off my own bus!" Damian shouted.

Jayson grabbed the Overlord by his other arm; together, Mom and Dad hoisted him down the stairs like they were taking out the trash. Jayson turned to Paulie, who was still sitting in the driver's seat, trying to blend into the background.

"You too, Albino Keith Richards. Out!"

"This is crazy, Jay," the Overlord complained. "You can't just leave us on the side of the road."

Jayson jumped to the bottom step, leaned out the door, and grabbed Damian by one of his leather lapels again. "Where's Sammy, Damian?" His voice was quavering with anger.

"I don't know where she is," Damian answered. His crooked little half-smile only made Jayson angrier.

"Don't lie to me!" he barked.

"I'm not lying, Jay. I don't know where she is."

"I think she might still be at the Gauntlet!" B.J. offered.

Dad whirled around to B.J. His chest was visibly rising and falling with every breath as he gazed at him in shock. "She's here?" He turned to Mom, and they fell into one of those silent conversations that B.J. could never decipher. "He brought her with him," Dad breathed, looking almost guilty. "I never thought he'd bring her, Di. If I'd known she was here, I would have..."

Mom grabbed his hand and squeezed it tenderly. "It's okay, Jayson. We had no way of knowing he'd bring her with him. We didn't believe anything Merv told us—we both know he's crazy."

"But she's here," Dad marveled. His guilty expression grew slowly into a passionate smile. "The Money's here."

B.J. studied his dad's proud smile, and it was suddenly all so clear...

Dad's song *was* about Sammy, just as she'd felt it was. He wasn't writing about someone stealing all his cash in Atlantic City; he was writing about someone stealing his *daughter*—the baby they had all nicknamed "the Money"—probably because they knew she'd grow up to be a superstar.

Now all the other clues were rushing into B.J.'s head: The way he'd felt so connected to Sammy from the moment they met—the way she looked so familiar. *Of course* she looked familiar. She had all the traits B.J. had never shared with his father: the light blond hair; the slim, chiseled face; the gray-green eyes.

And the *quilt.* The Overlord had said that Sammy wore only orange because it reminded of her of her baby blanket. But it wasn't a blanket. It was a *quilt.* A big bright orange quilt with the most confusing Bon Jovi quote in history. Dad wasn't worshipping a stupid quilt. He was keeping a constant reminder of his long-lost daughter.

"Dad, I think we can still find her!" Now B.J.'s chest was heaving with excitement too. "If we can get back to the Gauntlet, I think we can find her together!"

Dad locked his eyes with B.J.'s, and for the very first time, B.J. felt like his dad was looking at him man-to-man. "Well then, what are we waiting for, son?" Dad said.

★ ★ ★

"She's your daughter, isn't she?" B.J. was behind his dad's shoulder in the front seat. Mom was sitting next to him, and the band had all gathered close. "She's your daughter, and I'm his son."

Dad nodded as they sped back down Ocean Avenue.

"But how?" B.J. asked. "I know you hate 'the big questions,' Dad, but come on. You've got to give me something here. I'm completely lost."

"Me too," Kev said.

"Yuh-huh." Jann raised his hand in agreement.

"Me too," Layla agreed. "One hundred percent lost here."

"Diana...?" Dad called back to Mom. "I think he needs to hear it all now."

"I know," Mom agreed. She didn't look thrilled about it, but she took a deep breath and started filling in the missing pieces.

"We were all in a band together," she said. "It was called Bayonette. It was me and Damian and Jayson and Astrid."

"Astrid," B.J. said. "That's Sammy's mom."

B.J.'s mom nodded.

"Wait, *you* were in Bayonette?" It had taken B.J. a second to catch that part.

"It was another life, sweetie."

B.J. thought back to the old Bayonette picture at the Fire Pit. The bass player and drummer had so much hair in their faces, he'd automatically assumed they were dudes!

"We were two couples," Mom said. "Me and Damian were together and so were Jayson and Astrid."

"You and the Overlord, Mom? You were going out with that psycho?"

Mom bowed her head in shame. "He used to be *nice*," she insisted. "He wasn't always this crazy."

"He was pretty crazy," Dad interjected.

"Well, all right, but the man could *rock*, Jayson," Mom argued.

"Everyone was in love with him. I was *twenty years old.* It was the *nineties.* Nobody knew what they were doing in the nineties."

"*Chill*, woman," Dad laughed. "It's all good."

"Just finish the story, Mom," B.J. said. "How did me and Sammy end up with different dads?"

"Jayson and Astrid had Sambora," she explained. "And we all adored her and we all took care of her on tour. And then, a year later, Damian and I had you, Benjamin."

"It's okay, Mom," B.J. said. "You can stop calling me Benjamin. I know my real name now."

"Oh, all right," she sighed. "We had you…Bon Jovi. Ugh, what were we thinking?"

"Wait, your real name is Bon Jovi?" Kev giggled. The giggle turned into a chorus of laughter from the band.

"The *point* is," Mom cut in, "everything was absolutely fine until *Merv* showed up at one of our shows. He told us all about B.L.A.S.T. and their crazy prophecy. We all just laughed it off, but a few nights later, we found out that Damian had *believed* all of it. We found out in the worst possible way. He and Astrid disappeared with Sammy."

"In Atlantic City," B.J. said.

Mom looked shocked. "How did you know that?"

"Um," B.J. looked down. "The Overlord told me," he mumbled.

"Well, Damian had convinced Astrid that the road was no life for her daughter," Mom said. "He told her that he wanted to take her and Sammy to California, where they could settle down."

"She believed him," Dad said, shaking his head bitterly. "And she took the Money. That's what we used to call Sammy—the Money. Astrid took her away from me."

"But it was a trick," Mom said. "Settling down wasn't Damian's real plan. Two nights later, he stole Sammy from her crib in the hotel. All because he couldn't let there be a 'Sacred Two' without him in it." She took hold of B.J.'s hand. "He'd left me behind with you and Jayson, sweetie. I was so scared that these B.L.A.S.T. lunatics would try to take you too, so I asked Jayson if he would help me take care of you in Cleveland, where we could hide you from B.L.A.S.T. and make sure you never even *thought* about playing any rock and roll music or fulfilling their crazy prophecy." Mom reached over the partition and squeezed Jayson's shoulder. "And then, while we were taking care of you, we fell in love. And we got married. And Jayson became your father."

"But what about Astrid?" B.J. asked. "What happened to Sammy's mom?"

"She's in Texas," Dad said. "Astrid and I hardly even talk anymore. It's just too sad. There were four or five times when we almost got to Sammy, but she was always gone by the time we got there.

He always had them playing in these underground clubs, playing under different band names, never staying in the same place for more than a night. It was just impossible to keep track of them."

"She doesn't even know..." B.J. shook his head in quiet amazement. "Sammy doesn't even know that the Overlord isn't her real dad. She doesn't know that she's got a real dad looking for her and a mom waiting for her in Texas. We have to *find* her, Dad. We have to find Sammy and tell her. This is everything she's ever wanted."

"Oh, we'll find her," Dad said, leaning forward against the wheel. "If she's there, then we'll find her, son. Believe that."

"There's just one more thing," B.J. said.

"What's that?" Dad asked.

B.J. peered back at Layla, Kev, and Jann. With all hell breaking lose on the Over-Bus, he hadn't really gotten to check in on how much they still hated him. "Well..." he began tentatively, "if we're going back to the Gauntlet...then the band still has a chance to play."

"What band?" Dad asked.

"My band," B.J. said. "I think we still have a shot to win it." He glanced back at their faces. Layla had definitely cracked a smile, though she was trying to hide it. Kev couldn't hold a grudge for more than ten minutes—he was already grinning from ear to ear. The question mark was Jann.

"What do you think, Solo?" B.J. asked. "You want to help me try to win this thing? 'Cause I think we can win this thing."

Jann crossed his arms tightly over his chest. He kept the badass frown glued to his face as he gave B.J. the once over.

"Of course we're going to win this thing," he said. "We're the Good Supreme." He thrust out his fist to B.J. "Knock the rock, Bon Jovi."

B.J. smiled joyfully as they knocked and exploded the rock. "That's my name," he said. "Don't wear it out."

"Oh sweet!" KeVonne bellowed. "The Supreme is back in business, y'all! We need to start rehearsing. We only got a few hours till our slot."

"Yeah, I bet they left some instruments in here!" Layla jumped out of her seat, giving over to her total excitement.

"I know there's a few sweet guitars in the back," B.J. said. "This is going to be awesome!"

"Okay, *hold up* there, son." Jayson's booming voice cut through the flurry of activity and all heads turned in his direction. "I'm dying to see you play, Beej. I really am. Everyone at the Gauntlet was talking about the tall kid who blew them away at the Firepit, and I couldn't be prouder of what you've accomplished, but I think you're forgetting something."

"What?" B.J. asked.

"I think you're forgetting the rules," Dad said.

"No, I'm only going to play with the Good Supreme," B.J. replied. "Just one band."

"No, son, I'm talking about the *other* rule. A little something about playing an original song?" Dad locked eyes with B.J. in the rearview mirror. "They all said you'd played a song that sounded just like something I would have written back in the Bayonette days. Maybe there's something you want to tell your bandmates."

"Right," B.J. sighed. His shoulders slumped forward as he dropped back into his seat.

Kev turned to B.J., looking mildly concerned. "What's he talking about, Beej?"

B.J. shut his eyes with embarrassment. Now that he'd actually heard his father say he loved him, he felt even guiltier for stealing his song. He'd confessed all his lies to Sammy in the letter, but he still hadn't told the band the whole truth.

"'Atlantic City,'" he said, mumbling to the floor. "I didn't write it."

"What?" Layla's eyes filled with disappointment.

"It's my dad's song," he said. "I kind of cribbed it."

"Kind of?" Dad checked him in the rearview again.

"Okay, I totally and completely cribbed it."

"Oh, *dude*." KeVonne looked like he'd just witnessed a terrible accident.

"Seriously?" Jann dropped back down in his seat.

B.J.'s gut was throbbing and so was his head. "But the judges wouldn't have to know," he said. "They'll still think it's an original."

"Yeah, they wouldn't have to know," Dad said, "but it's like I always used to tell my band. If you want to be a real songwriter, then you've got to speak the Truth with a capital T. And singing my song just wouldn't be the Truth, son."

"I know," B.J. said. "Believe me, I know."

"Well, what about that 'Dog Wars' song?" Jann asked. "We could still win with that one."

"Oh, dude! You played 'Dog Wars' for an audience?" Dad was thrilled.

"Yeah," B.J. said.

"How'd it go?"

"They loved it," B.J. said, turning back to Jann. "Yeah, that one's his too."

"I knew that," Kev admitted.

Jann pounded his fist on his seat. "Okay, well, what *actual* original songs do you have, Levine? And do *not* say '911 Emergency Toast.'"

B.J. mulled over his tragic lack of original material, desperately scanning his memory banks for something—anything he might have come up with since the beginning of his musical career the week before.

"Well...there is one thing I was kind of working on," he said.

Layla grabbed his arm and pulled him up out of his seat. "Look, you can still do this, Levine. I know you can. Play us your song."

★ ★ ★

They were hunched over the kitchen table like a panel of teen judges, staring at B.J. expectantly, desperately, as he gazed down at a keyboard they'd found in the back of the bus. It was like the entire last week had never taken place—like they were all back in his Manhattan basement for the first time, waiting for him to show them his enormous talents.

Why had he told them there was "something he was kind of working on"? It wasn't even "something." It wasn't even a half or a third of something. It was closer to "nothing," but they were going onstage tonight and the clock was running out. This was B.J.'s Hail Mary pass—his blind, last-second heave into the skies, praying to the spirits of his namesakes—Misters Bon Jovi and Springsteen—to help him find the end zone.

He laid his index finger down on the keys and began to plunk.

Plunk plunk plunk plunk plunk plunk…

Then onto his second note.

Plunk plunk plunk plunk plunk plunk…

And then his third.

Plunk plunk plunk plunk plunk plunk…

And back to his first.

Plunk plunk plunk plunk plunk plunk...

He tried to add a fourth note, but that just tripped him up, so he began cycling the first three notes again, hoping for a sudden burst of genius.

Plunk plunk plunk plunk plunk plunk...

"Dude." Jann looked deeply unhappy. "What are you doing?"

"Well, that's as far as I've gotten," B.J. said.

"It's three notes," Jann said. "You're playing three notes."

"Well, I told you I was *working* on it. It's not like it's done."

"Not done? Not *done*? It's *three notes*." Jann stepped away from the kitchen table to better manage his frustration.

"It is kind of just three notes, Beej." Kev was at least trying to be polite about it.

"Wait, wait," B.J. grabbed Kev's shoulder. "There were some words too."

Why are you doing this? Those are not words. Do NOT sing them the "words" to this "song."

"Well, what are the words?" Layla asked, trying to encourage him, just as she always did.

"Okay, it's like..."

No, don't do it, Levine. But he did. He plunked and he sang...

I can only play three notes
I can only play three notes

I can only play three notes
Three notes is all I can play

"Okay, *stop.*" Jann's face was turning a deep shade of red. Even his eyes looked crimson, though that was probably B.J.'s imagination. "Those are the lyrics? *I can only play three notes?* You're calling that lyrics? What is that?"

B.J. gave the only answer he could think of. "That's the truth with a capital T. I can only play three notes. No…?" He banged his head down on the keys, producing a very dark and ugly chord.

"Okay, I'm out." Jann started for the front of the bus. "Let me off this bus, dude."

Layla jumped up and blocked his path. "No, Jann, you can't do that. You can't just walk out every time it's bad. Did you know that anything that was ever good started with something bad?"

"No, I didn't know that," Jann said.

"Well, it's true. But if you walk out on it in the beginning, then it just stays bad. So it's our job to sit here and make it good. And I think Levine's got something here."

B.J. popped his slightly bruised head up from the keyboard. "You do?"

"I do," Layla said.

He could see the thoughts begin to churn in the back of her

brilliant mind as her eyes narrowed with intensity. "Play it again," she said, pushing herself right up next to him at the keyboard.

He played what little of it there was for Layla again, and she began to bob her head to the nonexistent beat. Or maybe there was a beat in there that only a drummer could hear? A smile crept up in the corner of her mouth.

"It's a three-chord classic," she declared.

"It is?" B.J. still sounded like an idiot when he was sitting too close to Layla.

"It is," she said. "There's nothing wrong with a good three-chord classic, Levine. There's like a million of them—'Louie Louie,' 'Knockin' on Heaven's Door,' 'Brown Eyed Girl,' 'Wild Thing,' 'Save It for Later'—my personal favorite, 'Twist and Shout'—and almost everything the Ramones ever wrote. Should I go on, *Jann*?"

Jann bowed his head and stormed off to Sammy's bedroom. When he came back out, he was holding one of Sammy's vintage guitars in one hand and a bass for KeVonne in the other. "I like the Ramones," he said.

"Let's go, let's *go*." KeVonne smacked his hands together, grabbed the bass, and lowered his goggles into piloting position.

Layla started doubling B.J.'s three notes at the top of the keyboard and B.J. began to feel the faintest trace of something warm growing in his belly. He was reasonably sure that it was inspiration.

"Do you think you could play three chords instead of three notes?" she asked.

"I really can't," B.J. said, concentrating on playing the notes. "When I try to play chords, I need to use my pinky, and I get all messed up when I try to add the pinky."

"Well then, I'll just be the pinky," Layla said. She slid her hand down the keyboard and began to play the harmony to B.J.'s melody.

But B.J. had stopped playing altogether. "What did you just say?"

"I said I'd play the pinky. Why'd you stop?" Layla turned and noticed that B.J. was now staring at her like she was either a god or a ghost.

"No, that's not what you said. You said you'd *be* the pinky." He slid back and took a better look at Layla as Terry the Wünder-Dwarf's exact words came rushing back:

...The one who inspires the front man. The one who believes in him no matter what. Who helps him bring all his songs to life...

"It's you," B.J. breathed.

"Me what?"

"You're the pinky. It was never Sammy. It was *you.*"

Maybe Merv wasn't crazy. Maybe Merv and Terry and Chicken Fingers and Tiffani and the rest of B.L.A.S.T. weren't crazy at all. They were right about B.J.'s Sacred Pinky. They just had the wrong pinky.

B.J. felt a whopping moment of clarity coming on.

"You guys…we're going to win this thing."

CHAPTER thirteen

All the panic was gone. As he looked out at two thousand bikers and rockers and freaks and misfits, all piled like sardines into the amphitheater, he felt an overwhelming sense of calm. Because there was no more doubt. He knew who he was and he knew why he had come here.

"Good evening, New Jersey!" he howled into the mic.

"*WOOOOOOOOOOOOO!*" The singular sound of a rabid Jersey crowd rose high into the clear—though mildly polluted—indigo sky.

He felt the hot spotlight burning his forehead and his prominent nose, and it was good.

"My name," he said, hearing his voice echo across an ocean of bandannas, "is Bon Jovi Springstein!"

This brought out a cheer of such brute force that it was like a giant hand shoving his wiry frame back against the drum kit. He laughed heartily with Jann, Kev, and Layla and climbed through the wall of noise back to the mic.

"People of Bayonne and Monmouth County, and the greater tristate area…I have come here to the Holy Land of Asbury Park for one reason and one reason only. And that is to *rock your faces!*"

"*YAAAAAAAAHHHHHHHHHHHHHHHH!*"

The decibel level was so high that their piercing, animal roar turned into a deep, distorted rumbling in B.J.'s eardrums. But he was not frightened.

He pulled the mic stand to the piano and began to plunk his three notes. And as he plunked, their faces grew confused. But he was still not frightened. Because as he began to sing, he knew he was doing the one and only thing that mattered. He was speaking the Truth with a capital T.

I can only play three notes
I can only play three notes
I can only play three notes
Three notes is all I can play…

I can only play three notes
I only know three notes
I can only play three notes
There's nothin' else I can say…

They began to laugh, but that was of no concern to Bon Jovi Springstein because he knew that the Truth could be funny at times. And sure enough, when Jann Solo hammered out his first fuzzy, distorted chord, their laughter fell away and their heads began to bob to Layla the Whala's booming backbeat and KeVonne HaMonde's chunky, funky bass. B.J. pulled the mic from its stand and leaped from the piano, flying downstage toward the crowd.

But I can sing. Sing this song.
Over and over. All day long.
'Cause I can only play three notes, it's all I can do
But if I only know three notes, I'll play them for you. HOOOOOOOO

Jann laid in some crunchy soloing with the three chords, and by the time they took it down for the sensitive part of the song, the Good Supreme had them eating out of their hands.

This is the sensitive part of my only song.
It's sensitive, so sensitive, is sensitive so wrong?

I wish I could write you pretty, pretty love, love songs
And blow your mind with blinding lightning white hot solos

But I can only play three notes. It's all I can say
And if I only know three notes, I'll play them all day
I only know three notes. It's all I can do
But if I only know three notes, I'll play them for you. HOOOOOOO

This was B.J.'s moment. Whether the crowd knew it or not, they were witnessing history. And one day, years from now, they would tell their kids that they were there on the very evening when B.J. Levine, aka Nigel "Hot Wings" Thunderdome, aka Bon Jovi Springstein became a full-on, fire-breathing MEGALORD OF RRRRRROCK.

★ ★ ★

Dear Nigel aKa B.J.,

I'm hoping that Burrito Butt will find you after the show and give you this note because they promised me they would.

I am so sorry I missed you, Nigel (sorry, but you'll always be Nigel to me). Right after my dad chased you off, he went ballistic on me and told me we were leaving the Gauntlet. He gave me this long lecture about how I needed to stay away from you at all costs. I still don't understand why he's so obsessed with Keeping me away from you. It's almost like he's scared of you or something. It sounds like he is so obsessed with you that he had our manager and bus driver Paulie following you around? Did my dad somehow know you before the Fire Pit? Is that even possible? And who are these B.L.A.S.T. people chasing you around? This Merv person sounds quite terrifying and I will definitely watch out for him—thanks for the heads up.

I don't know, Nigel. I think there's a lot of things going on here that I just don't understand. I can only hope that you are safe now, wherever you are. As for me, I think I'm going to be okay. I'm not sure, but I think so.

I couldn't let my dad take me away again. Not this time. When he said we were leaving the Gauntlet, I just ran away and found a spot where I knew he wouldn't find me. I had to hide there for a while, and by the time I made it back to the dumpster, you were gone. I started to get so sad that I'd lost you, especially with the lead singer of Burrito Butt singing this terrible song about surrendering to the doom of chains. But then he gave me your letter.

I just want you to know that you are NOT a lousy writer, Nigel. Your letter was honest and true and it made me understand so many things. I know I've gotta get out of this place and find my mom, even if I don't have a dime, and I know that because of you.

You were so scared of everything at first. You were scared of your new school and scared of your band and scared of singing in front of people, but no matter how scared you were, you just went ahead and did it all. You did all the things that scared you the most, and that's how I want to be. I want to be like you, Nigel, except not fake British.

So I've decided to hit the road on my own. The rest of the Overlord band said they'd come with me and watch over me and play shows with me. It turns out they hated playing with my dad just as much as I did. We're going to gig our way across the country, starting at the Fire Pit, and we're going to try to find my mom. It'll be a long and winding road, I know, but the truth is, Nigel, I already feel like I'm halfway there. You know...livin' on a prayer. That's how we do.

I know I'll find you out there somewhere. Somehow, I just know that I'll see you again, so I don't need to be sad. I'll just listen for your song.

Your friend (definitely forever),
Sambora Springstein

Dear Sammy,

Hi, it's me, Nigel, aka B.J., again. YES, Burrito Butt found me after the show and gave me your letter, and it told me the one and only thing I needed to know. You're going to be at the Fire Pit tonight! And we are going to find you there, so stay put.

I have money for you, Sammy. We won it at the Gauntlet, and I'm going to bring you my share! I also know that your mother is in Texas and that your dad is really my dad and that my dad is really your dad, so—

Okay, I'm going too fast again. Sorry, I'm just a little excited—I mean, okay, I'm crazy excited. It's been quite a night.

Why am I even writing you this letter? It doesn't really make any sense because I can't actually give you the letter until we get to the Fire Pit and then I can just tell you everything I'm telling you now. But I'm sitting here, looking out the window of the Overlord's bus, racing to get to you, and I can't really wait to tell you everything, so I'll just have to tell you twice. Do I sound crazy? I feel a little crazy right now. But good crazy.

My dad finally saw me play. And I think he was impressed! We've decided that once we pick you up at the Fire Pit, we're all going to hit a few more clubs and play a few gigs together before I have to go back to school on Monday. I think it's called a supergroup, but I'm not completely sure. My dad is super psyched because all he's really wanted to do for the last thirteen years is play some rock and roll music on the road again. I tried to convince my mom to play with us too, but she says that the only thing a great rock band truly needs is a good accountant, so she's sticking with her day job.

There's a lot more I need to tell you, but I think for now, I'll just put it like this:

I ride this bus, a loaded six-string in the seat next to me

I play for keeps, but I'll definitely be back by Monday

I've been to Cleveland, New York, Stroudsburg, Philadelphia, and Asbury Park. And I'm extremely tall.

I've seen between two and three thousand faces.

And I've rocked at least two thousand and fifteen of them.

Only nine hundred and ninety-seven thousand, nine hundred and eighty-five faces to go. Give me a few years. I'll get there.

Your friend forever,
Bon Jovi Springstein (I'll explain later)

About the Author

Barnabas Miller has written many books for children and young adults. His most recent young adult novel, *7 Souls*, was published in July 2010. He also composes and produces music for film and network television. He lives in New York City with his wife, Heidi; their cat, Ted; and their dog, Zooey.